I0742077

THE PANAY INCIDENT

(A roman à clef)

Captain S. Martin Shelton, USNR (Ret.)

Inquiries should be addressed to the publisher
Lamplight Press
PO Box 82516
Austin, Texas 78708

ISBN: 978-0-9979774-9-3

Printed in the United States of America
by Lightning Source

DEDICATION

I dedicate this book to those unsung and heroic American sailors, marines, and civilians who manned the China Station during the chaos that suffused throughout China in the 1910s, 1920s, and 1930s. With undaunted courage and wholehearted dedication they protected our citizens, diplomatic personnel, and commercial interests during the turmoil in the Celestial Kingdom.

Ding Hoa!

ACKNOWLEDGEMENT

I recognize the following professionals who were instrumental in the publication of this narrative:

Danielle Hartman Acee for her sage counsel and expertise in finessing this manuscript through the publication process

Doug Brown for his exceptional cover and character artwork

Michal Cox for his skilled photo shopping of the images

Samantha Johnson (*nom de plume*) for her eagle-eye editing of this manuscript

Chief Photographer's Mate Joseph Kirschbaum, USN, (Ret.), technical advisor

Lieutenant Commander Ralph Lewis, USN (Ret.), technical advisor

Senior Chief Photographer's Mate Tim Timmerman, USN (Ret.), technical advisor

AUTHOR'S NOTES

Throughout this narrative, I endeavored to maintain military, historical, and geographical accuracy. I've used the *USS Panay* ship company's real names whenever possible. However, the storyteller, Chief Radioman Matthew Marne, is a fictional character. I've added fictional activities that are not in the official record to keep the narrative empathetic and coherent. Please review the Historical Background at the end of the book for additional information related to this *roman à clef.*

The official Navy record of the Japanese naval aircraft attack on the gunboat *USS Panay, PR-5,* is the primary source for the data I've used in developing this narrative. However, sometimes this Navy record's details differ from the open-source accounts. For example, the Navy says that "Three large Japanese twin motor planes … attacked the *Panay."* Most of the other sources agree that there were four Yokuska single-engine aircraft that carried out the attack. There are other discrepancies, but no need to list them here. In my narrative, I've used those facts that I believe are rational within the frame of my naval experience. Your concurrence, please. I've added an asterisk after key persons and equipment when first mentioned in the text to alert the reader to their images in the Photographic Gallery starting on page 182.

I've used the Wade-Giles Romanization (spelling) of geographic and personnel names—as was the custom at the time.* (2) The Chinese did not like this spelling and pronunciation because they did not reflect accurately the Mandarin language syntax. Accordingly, the People's Republic of China introduced the Hanyu Pinyin spelling in 1958. For example, "Peiping" became "Beijing" and "Canton" became "Guangzhou."

Note 1. On Sunday, 12 December 1937, at 1338 hours, in an unprovoked attack, Japanese naval airplanes bombed and strafed the American gunboat *United States Ship Panay*—sinking it, killing two sailors, and wounding most of its crew.* (3)

Note 2. On Sunday, 7 December 1941, at 0755 hours, in an unprovoked attack, Japanese naval airplanes bombed, strafed, and torpedoed United States Navy ships in Pearl Harbor, Hawaii—sinking 5 battleships* (4) and inflicting 3,200 casualties.* (5)

ADDENDA

ONE

*Midstream, Yangtze River, near Shanghai, China,
0932 hours, Sunday, 12 December 1937*

The artillery shell exploded in the Yangtze about fifty yards from my ship, the gunboat *USS Panay*. I heard shrapnel pinging off our steel hull. A fusillade of machine-gun bullets whizzed by our starboard side and ripped into the river. Stray bullets continued to fly around us and errant shells exploded in the river close aboard.

Whoa! Before I get too deeply into this narrative, I'd best introduce myself. I'm your narrator, Chief Radioman Matthew Marne, United States Navy,* (6) ship's company the gunboat *USS Panay*.

To continue: The Japanese Kwangtung Army siege of Nanking, China's capital, raged on in full force.* (7)

The *Panay* was on station in this Chinese river to safeguard Western business interests and to protect American diplomatic personnel.

Lieutenant Commander James J. Hughes, our skipper, intent on getting the *Panay* out of the fire zone, ordered Chief Boatswain Mate Earnest Halhmann, the deck bosun, to weigh anchor. As soon as the anchor broke water, Hughes directed the lee helmsman, Seaman Stanley McEowen, "Dead slow ahead."

In turn, McEowen responded, "Aye, skipper, dead slow ahead." He grabbed the dual handles of the engine room telegraph,* (8) pushed them forward to the STOP, and pulled them back until the indicators were on the "dead slow ahead" position. The telegraph's bells rang persistently. Within moments we were moving upriver.

"Helmsman, steer midstream." (That was Seaman William Lander.)

"Aye, aye, skipper." Lander checked the rudder-angle indicator, turned the helm wheel three degrees port, and reported, "Midstream, sir."

"Navigator, plot a course for Wuhu." (Chief Quartermaster John Lang)

"Aye, sir. To Wuhu."

I felt the vibrations of our dual steam engines through the deck. I was standing on the port side, near the quarterdeck, and saw Nanking in flames. I could not reckon the chaos inside China's capitol, or the brutal horrors the Japanese troops were inflicting on Chinese citizens.* (9)

To ensure that the belligerents knew the *Panay* was a neutral ship, we had sewn several large American flags onto canvas awnings topside, and were flying a very large flag from the mast and a smaller one on the aft gaff.* (10)

We were headed about twenty-five miles upriver. The skipper tasked me to send the movement message to Admiral Harry E. Yarnell, commander of the Asiatic Fleet.* (11) Additional addressees were the Japanese senior naval commander, Rear Admiral Mitsunamni Teizo,* (12) and General Tang Shengyshi,* (13) commander of Chinese forces. I sent copies to the two British gunboats close by, *HMS Ladybird** (14) and *HMS Bee,** (15) and to the several Standard Oil Socony Vacuum Company river tankers anchored nearby.* (16)

Late in the afternoon of the previous day, the last four consular members remaining in Nanking had boarded the *Panay.* At around 0700 hours, ten American civilians boarded. Included were newsreel cameramen, print journalists, and several foreign correspondents. Also onboard were a number of Chinese government officials and businessmen escaping the terror inside Nanking.

Shortly, the three Standard Oil Socony Vacuum Company river tankers, *Mei Ping,** (17) *Mei Hsia,* and *Mei An,* got underway and followed us astern. Onboard were company employees and their families, and escaping Chinese civilians. All three tankers displayed many large American flags, horizontally and vertically. Following those were the British gunboats *HMS Ladybird* and *HMS Bee.* Uninvited, but welcome nonetheless, dozens of junks joined the convoy.* (18) They were loaded with escaping Chinese and their belongings.

Two

*US Navy Hospital, Subic Bay, Commonwealth of the Philippines,
1400 hours, 28 December 1937*

Reckon I ought to back up and start at the beginning to establish some coherence to this narrative. I'm a patient in the US Navy Hospital, Subic Bay,* (19) Commonwealth of the Philippines, recovering from wounds inflicted during that unprovoked Japanese naval aircraft attack on my ship, the gunboat *USS Panay*—now resting on the bottom of the Yangtze.

This morning, Admiral Harry E. Yarnell visited the *Panay* survivors' ward. He presented the Purple Heart* (20) to all my shipmates on the ward, and bestowed the Silver Star* (21) and Bronze Star with Combat "V"* (22) upon a host of our crew for gallantry in action. He conferred the Navy Cross* (23) upon twenty-one of my shipmates.

I saw the Admiral and his aide approaching my bed. I tried to rise on one elbow, without success. He spoke in his raspy, commanding voice. "Chief Matthew Marne, lie still. No need for naval formalities now. Your commanding officer report tells me you, though suffering serious wounds in your back, arms, and legs from bomb shards and splinters, kept the Panay's radio operating. When machine-gun bullets disabled the radio and inflicted additional wounds, you manned a machine gun and fought with steadfast courage. I am proud to award you the Navy Cross for unstinting bravery in action. Congratulations." He also pinned a Purple Heart with a bronze oak leaf cluster* (24) on my robe. The Admiral snapped a salute to all and said, "Men, your sterling bravery and dauntless courage were in keeping with the best traditions of the Naval Service. All hands in the Asiatic Squadron and in the Pacific Fleet send you their 'Well done.'"

As Admiral Yarnell started to depart our ward, Chief Boatswain Mate Halhmann formed a ten-man 'tending the side' from the ambulatory patients. The men stood at attention, or something close to it, in two parallel, facing rows and saluted. Chief Quartermaster John Lang commandeered a call bell from the chief nurse and, in lieu of a ship's bell, rang it four times. Chief Halhmann piped the admiral 'over the side' with his bosun pipe* (25) and Gunner's Mate Second Class John Hennessy, in his raspy voice, announced, "Commander Asiatic Fleet departing."

Our rendering of honors was not quite in accord with naval regulations. But as the admiral walked between our rows, I saw him crack a faint smile as he returned our honors with a salute.

The Navy also awarded all hands the Navy Expeditionary Medal* (26) and the China Service Medal.* (27)

THREE

US Navy Hospital, Subic Bay, Commonwealth of the Philippines,
1530 hours, 28 December 1937

All's quiet 'round here now. I ought to start at the beginning of this story—to set the stage for that Japanese sneak attack on my ship. I want all Americans to know exactly what happened on that fateful day of 12 December 1937. And, since I'm your narrator, you ought to know some details about me.

I'm from Marfa, Texas, a small town on US Highway 90, about 400 miles west of San Antonio. I graduated from Alpine High School in 1915, and started my college education at Sul Ross Normal College in Alpine.* (28) After completing my first two semesters, I declared a major in electrical engineering. I was looking forward to a career in a profession that would be challenging and fulfilling.

Unfortunately, the Great War* (29) was raging throughout the world. On paper, the United States was neutral; however, we supported, *sub rosa,* the Triple Entente—Great Britain,* (30) France,* (31), Italy,* (32)—and their Allies with all manner of war materials, POL (petroleum, oil, lubricants), medical supplies, and foodstuffs.

On 1 February 1917, Germany* (33) resumed its unrestricted submarine warfare* (34)—sinking several of our merchant ships. On 1 March 1917, President Wilson* (35) announced that the U.S. was breaking diplomatic relations with Germany. Two days later a German U-boat attacked and sank our liner the *SS Housatonic.* * (36) Accordingly, political tensions rose precipitously. Increasing the disquiet was the German Foreign Ministry's encoded "Zimmerman telegram"* (37) incident in mid-March 1917. British intelligence (Secret Intelligence Service, MI6*) (38) intercepted this message and cryptographers decoded it: Germany had encouraged Mexico* (39) to invade Texas* (40) and the other southwestern states should the United States declare war on Germany and the Central Powers. Incensed, President Wilson, on 2 April 1917, asked Congress to declare war on Germany.* (41)

Determined to get involved in the fight, I enlisted in the Navy.* (42) After boot camp in San Diego, at my request, I got orders to report to Radioman's A school on Treasure Island in San Francisco Bay. On graduation four months later, I was promoted to Seaman Radioman Striker* (43) and ordered to report to the *USS Porter*) a ship of the Eighth Division, Destroyer Force, Atlantic Fleet.* (44)

To summarize, my ship spent the Great War in the North Sea: laying mines, escorting ships of the line, and hunting *unterseeboots*. About halfway into our cruise, the Navy promoted me to Radioman Third Class.* (45) We killed one U-boat* (46) in early March and fired at the LZ32 Zeppelin* (47) in May with no apparent damage. Our routine continued unabated until the Armistice on 11 November 1918. On return to the United States, my skipper, Lieutenant Commander Warne Workman, recommended me for the Bronze Star medal* (48) for meritorious achievement. I was hooked.

I decided then and there on a twenty-year career. It would be a great opportunity to expand my experience, visit exotic ports worldwide, earn promotions, attend additional radio and leadership schools, and earn a handsome retirement while still a relatively young fellow. My goal, on retirement, was to attend Texas Tech University* (49) and earn that electrical engineering degree.

On our return to Hampton Roads, Virginia, I signed a four-year enlistment contract. The Radioman detailer at the BUPERS (Bureau of Personnel) cut orders for me to report to Naval Intelligence Headquarters in Washington, DC, and included a thirty-day leave.

FOUR

My home, Marfa, Texas, February 1919

At home, my parents, much to my chagrin, treated me as the returning conquering hero. Nonetheless, my time in Marfa was well spent: visiting with classmates, attending a rodeo, and hunting in the Davis Mountains* (50)—I got a twelve-point buck. I made several journeys to the Big Bend area to view the scenery* (51) and take photographs with my Kodak Brownie camera.* (52)

One Saturday, two of my high school pals, Jesse and Roybob, piled into Jesse's flivver* (53) and drove to Presidio on the Rio Grande. We crossed the river to party at the *Bueno Tempo* establishment in Ojinaga, Mexico—legal Canadian booze, great steaks, lilting Latin music, and dancing the Charleston with delightful flappers.* (54) My pals visited the bawdyhouse. Not I. I may be dumb but I am not stupid.

Young readers may wonder why we went to Mexico to imbibe in "legal" alcohol beverages. Prohibition, it was. The eighteenth Amendment to our Constitution prohibited the sale of alcohol libations within the US of A.

I dated an ol' flame from my Sul Ross days—Eugenia Maria Barrister, a dynamite woman of many talents. She was twenty years old and gracefully tall and slender, with a darkly tanned, comely face, rich auburn hair cascading over her shoulders, bright green eyes that sparkled when pleased, and she blossomed where a woman ought to blossom.

She helped her widowed dad, Anthony (Tony) Barrister, run the several thousand acres of Pinto Canyon Ranch* (55) in the Chinati Mountains.* (56) Eugenia rode with her dad and the cowboys during roundup of white-face cattle,* (57) branded the calves,* (58) strung barbed-wire fences,* (59) and busted broncos.* (60)

I reckon we were an item. *Mui compatible*, as it were. Movies in Alpine, rodeos in Sanderson, quail hunting in the Davis Mountains,* (61) hiking in the Del Norte Mountains, and exploring the ghost town Pueblo Nuevo* (62) in the Big Bend area. Naturally, we packed side arms—to shoo away mountain lions,* (63) discourage *banditos*, and dispatch those venomous diamondbacks* (64)—which we did aplenty. Eugenia carried her Smith and Wesson 38 six-shooter, model 1905.* (65) I carried my 1911 Colt 45, my weapon of choice.* (66)

Toward the end of my leave, Eugenia and I were courting in the game room at the ranch—sipping bootleg rye whisky, dancing, laughing, and having the best of times. Reckon we did a touch more sipping than we ought. We starting "sparking" and then some serious "sparking." Mind you, don't jump to erogenous conclusions. Sparking, nothing seriously untoward. Nonetheless, Eugenia was ready to visit the Baptist minister in Alpine for the ceremony, and make me a cowboy.

Fortunately a *deus ex machina* saved my fantail—not a Greek god in white robes, but a U.S. sailor in his blue uniform. BUPERS (Navy's Bureau of Personnel) sent telegraphic orders that cancelled my leave and ordered me to report *post haste* to Naval Intelligence Headquarters. That afternoon, in my dress blues, I was on the train to San Antonio and New Orleans, and onward to Washington, DC. I had time to kiss my parents *adios* and to send a letter to Eugenia trying to explain my feelings for her, and the difficult choice I had made to continue my Navy career.

FIVE

Naval Intelligence Headquarters, Washington, DC,
1530 hours, March 1919

The Special Security Officer administered the oath. I was now cleared for Top Secret, Sensitive Compartmented Information (SCI). I dealt with communications from our world-wide cadre of attachés. Generally, I worked the midnight shift, when most of the traffic arrived. No need to detail all my assignments—not relevant.

What's relevant to this narrative is that starting in March 1922, I attended Radioman "B" School, a year-long electronic and intelligence school that covered all manner of routine and non-routine subjects, and topics I'd never heard of. I graduated with a 3.9 average (4.0 is the highest score), and I earned the promotion to Radioman Second Class.* (67)

The Director of Naval Intelligence sent me to Naval Radiographic Unit 302 in Pearl Harbor, Territory of Hawaii. For the next two years, I traveled Pacific Oceana and the Far East on Temporary Additional Duty orders on various intelligence assignments at sea and ashore. Once, between assignments, I visited the folks in Marfa for a few days.

In May 1925, my intelligence detailer cut orders sending me to Texas A & M University for twenty-four months as a special student.* (68) Some sadist had devised my curriculum; it was sundry and irrational, or so I reckoned. Here are the highlights: logic, electronics, differential equations, Asian history, English literature, rhetoric, communications, and all manner of subjects that seemed to me to be irrelevant. For instance, someone at NAVINT dragooned me into a two-semester philosophy course. I didn't have much interest in what John Locke, Confucius, or Voltaire pontificated on, so nearly flunked—and that would have been the end of my naval career. The professors generously posted a "gentleman's C" grade for me. (I owe Doctor Professor what's-his-name a case of bootleg booze.) On the whole, I did okay. Earned a 3.8 grade average—that includes a 4.0 in vector analysis. My intelligence detailer sent a telegram with congratulations, informing me that I was promoted to Radioman First Class.* (69)

My next assignment was to the Naval Attaché in Canberra, Australia. (Down Under, as the "diggers" and the proud progeny of British prisoners say with great pride.) Nothing is routine in this small continent. The Aussies are great people: friendly, industrious, and warrior-like when irritated—much like west Texans. My "Green Door" assignments required travel throughout the continent, from Perth to Carnes, Adelaide to Darwin, Sydney to the remote outback. Saw the saltwater crocodiles,* (70) and wallabies,* (71) and had a close encounter with that deadly venomous serpent, the Eastern Taipan.* (72) I survived, the reptile did not. Had to reload my 1911 Colt 45.

In mid-February '29, I was enrolled in Cryptographic School on Treasure Island, California. For the next six months it was total immersion in the arcane machinations of code breaking. Much to my surprise, I found that I had an intuitive talent for this esoteric art.

On graduation, I had earned 30-days leave and I hightailed it to Texas. I left the Sunset Limited* (73) in El Paso and bought a Chrysler four-door, model 72 automobile.* (74) The next day, mom and dad met me in El Paso. I took them to the Barnum & Bailey's Greatest Show on Earth* (75)—it was wonderfully entertaining. On the five-hour drive to Marfa, we did lots of "catching up." At home, I didn't do much: read, visited old friends, hiked in the Davis Mountains, and rode Roybob's horse, Sally, several times. Signed the title of the Chrysler over to dad. I asked Jesse about Eugenia. He fudged and stumbled a bit. Eventually he said, "Several years ago, she married Gaylord Mackeson, a cattle broker out of Sanderson. Last time I saw her, she was okay. Haven't seen her lately. I saw Mackeson in Sanderson several months ago. We chatted a few minutes about the bull he was buying."

"Thanks, Jesse."

✳ ✳ ✳ ✳ ✳

In September 1929, I was at Naval Intelligence Headquarters, assigned to a special detail operating in a secure location in Crystal Spring, Maryland. 'Nuff said.

Promotions were slow in the peacetime Navy, especially during the Great Depression.* (76) Nonetheless, in October 1930 I passed the fleet-wide examinations for chief petty officer, with an exceptionally high score. A month later I was at headquarters with the director of naval intelligence. Captain Hayne Ellis* (77) assembled his staff, shook my hand, and said, "Congratulations, Chief Marne, your promotion to chief petty officer is well deserved." He presented me with the gold patch shoulder,* (78) chief petty officer's flat hat,* (79) and a string of three gold stripes* (80) (one stripe for each four years of good conduct service). The administrative officer gave me a check to purchase my chief's uniforms* (81) —they were more like a business suit than the "cracker jack" uniform I'd been wearing since 1917.* (82)

When my tour at NAVINT was over in January '31, I asked my detailer for orders to a fleet assignment. Naval intelligence sent me orders not to the Pacific fleet but to the University of Hawaii as a student in a total immersion course in the Japanese language. On Captain Ellis' direction, the administrative officer at headquarters had enrolled me as a special student under the *nom de guerre* Edward Ruhnke—a electrical engineer from Flagstaff, Arizona. And I had the documentation to prove it: birth certificate, high school record, and college transcript from the University of Arizona in Tucson, plus personal and business letters with the Flagstaff postal cancellation.

There were five other students in this class: two men of indeterminate age and three young women—all of Oriental heritage, perhaps Nisei. In no way did we socialize. In fact, I knew only their cover names: James, Paul, Jane, Liz, and Betty. One of the fellows wore a black patch over his left eye, and he walked awkwardly with a cane. The other fellow was short and stooped, and his deep black eyes saw your soul. The females. Indeed, the females. They were young, exquisitely attractive in all ways, shrewdly intelligent, keenly sharp-witted, and sophisticated to a fare-thee-well.

I've been in the green-door business long enough not to ask dumb questions and was aware enough to understand the ruse extant. Perhaps, at this late date, I should reveal the ruse. For now, I won't. And no questions. Nonetheless, I would suggest a reflection on this scenario. Sip slowly your chilled white wine, quaff your Foster's, or taste that shot glass of Kentucky's finest. Reflect. Let your mind wander. (Pause.) Got it? Indeed, you are correct.

The Japanese language course was challenging and demanded my total commitment. No social life whatsoever. Nothing but mastering those (expletives deleted) glyphs* (83) Nonetheless, I did it! Nine months later, I had completed the course with a 3.8 average. I had my suitcases packed, my ticket for the next day's Pan American World Airways China Clipper* (84) flight to Oakland, and I headed for thirty days leave in Marfa.

❊ ❊ ❊ ❊ ❊

The following month, I was en route to San Diego to report to the battleship *USS Arizona** (85) as ship's company for a two-year tour. We sailed throughout the Pacific, visiting ports, participating in fleet exercises, and skirting the boundary of Japan's secretive "Bamboo Curtain," covering a vast area of Micronesia.* (86) My assignment was entirely behind the "Green Door."

In October 1932, the naval intelligence detailer cut my tour on the *USS Arizona* short, and sent me to Nicaragua. My task was to provide tactical ELINT (Electronic Intelligence) to Marine Captain Lewis "Chesty" Puller, USMC* (87) and his Company M. The Marines were engaged in bandit suppression and in sorties against the Sandinista Marxist guerillas* (88) operating out of the San Cristóbal Mountains. I wore the standard Marine field uniform and carried my 1911 Colt 45. Several times, I had to fire my weapon at threatening Sandinistas.

For example, on 24 December 1932, we were pursuing a troop of Sandinistas on a steep mountain trail. A fellow burst out of the underbrush, emptied his *pistola* into the mule carrying my radio equipment, and lunged at me with his machete. I whirled to my right as he swung. The machete cut a small piece of muscle off my left arm. I put two 45 rounds in his chest. Our corpsman poured disinfectant into the cut (damn, that hurt!), and bandaged it. "Chief, you'll live. But keep that arm in the sling."

Captain Puller approached. "You killed that son-of-a-bitch. Nice goin.'" He retrieved the Sandinista's machete, stuck it in his belt, and started to leave. Over his shoulder he shouted, "Arm okay, chief? That's fine. I'll write you up for the Purple Heart."* (89) He headed up the trail.

I stayed in Nicaragua until January 1933, when President Franklin Roosevelt* (90) ordered all operations in Nicaragua ended. Captain Puller recommended me for the Bronze Star with Combat V device.* (91)

In February 1933, I was back at Headquarters working on contingency operation orders. Basically, I was milling about smartly, counting paper clips, and chafing for another fleet assignment. Not to be, however. Naval intelligence had other plans.

I boarded the Pan American World Airways China Clipper* (92) the next day, headed to Hong Kong. The naval intelligence detailer had cut orders for me to report incognito to the Naval Attaché in the British Crown Colony Singapore.* (93) Now I was Mister George Zimmerman, a dealer in rare earth elements from Trona, California, (94) and I had the paperwork to prove it. My reading material on the clipper was a custom-designed briefing on thulium, cerium, ytterbium and all the rest.

Egads! I was going to school again. Enough! I was ready to join the fleet. This time, naval intelligence had registered me in the National University of Singapore as a special student.* (95) My single course was full-time instruction in Mandarin.

As I exited the Seletar Airport concourse two Occidental fellows in tailor-made three-piece suits approached. The tall one extended his hand and said, "Good afternoon, Mister Zimmerman. Welcome to Singapore." The Aussie accent was noticeable.

I'd been in this Crown Colony twenty minutes and the funny business had already started. With false bravado, I greeted these fellows,

"And a good afternoon to you chaps from the British Secret Intelligence Service."* (96)

Before I could continue, the tall Aussie said, "Your suitcases are en route to the Raffles Hotel.* (97) Come with us. We'll drive you to the hotel."

No need to relay the details of our conversation. Suffice to say, I was given the ground rules for my conduct. Prudence was foremost. Cavort only with Commonwealth 'sheilas' ('dames' in the Aussie's Queen's English) and only after MI6 gave the okay. I got the short briefing on the intrigue extant in this international city, and was made an honorary associate of British Secret Intelligence Service.

I reported to Commander James Fleet, the Naval Attaché in the American Embassy. He endorsed my orders and said, to paraphrase, "Carry on; let me know from time to time how goes it."

In this class were three fellows of Oriental heritage—no names, no fraternization, no nothing. Study and practice in drawing glyphs was the Plan of the Day. No dames. Learning those glyphs was a tiger.* (98) Eventually, I had mastered about two thousand and I could read the local Chinese newspaper with a modicum of proficiency.* (99) Speaking Mandarin correctly was even more difficult. I must admit that I had almost mastered the five tones of the Mandarin spoken language—almost, but not fully. Nonetheless, in late December 1934, I completed the course with certificates of basic competency in Mandarin. Not bad for a good ol' boy from West Texas.

I had a great time in Marfa enjoying my thirty-day leave at Christmas time. Visiting with the folks, palling around with chums, hunting, reading, and goofing off. Jesse cautioned me not to contact Eugenia. And dad told me the details of the mountain lion attack that killed Eugenia's dad, Tony Barrister.

Far too soon, I was onboard the Pan American China Clipper headed for the Celestial Kingdom. I must admit that traveling first class can be addictive. My assignment was to the Naval Attaché's office in our embassy in Nanking, Republic of China.* (99A) Can't discuss the details of this assignment, but it was extraordinarily challenging, and required my complete dedication. I can tell you that I did frequent and extensive travel, often to the borders of Manchukuo* (100) and the People's Republic of Mongolia.* (101) Several times, I journeyed deep into Sinkiang Province in northwestern China.* close to the border of the Union of Soviet Socialist Republics.* Check my map of Sinkiang Province, China,* (102) in the Photographic Gallery, and make your own conclusions.

Chaos reigned in the Republic of China: bandits, warlord mercenaries,* (103) and renegade soldiers roamed almost unfettered throughout the countryside. Generalissimo Chang Kai-shek's national government was impotent* (104)—crippled by incompetence, corruption, partisanship, and a prejudicial judiciary. I carried my 1911 Colt 45, and two armed Marines accompanied me. We traveled in mufti and posed as representatives of the Genesis Geological Exploration Company.

Our guide and major domo on all our sojourns was Mister Charlie Chu. He was tall, slender, of indeterminate age, and loquacious to a crippling fault. He worked as a freelance contractor for the American Embassy. He carried a knife that resembled a Bowie knife and he knew how to use it.* (105) For instance, one time we were hiking along the Yuan (Red) River, deep in southern Kwangsi Province. Okay, I'll tell you. We were after ELINT (electronic intelligence) on Ho Chi Minh's Communist Viet Minh activities in French Indochina.

The brush was thick and I was using a machete to clear a trail. Mister Chu was behind me. Following were the Marines, the drovers, and the mules carrying our equipment. I did not step on that cobra but almost. He (she or it) raised its head and was ready to strike.* (106) Chu flicked his knife and in an instant that serpent was headless.

Whoops! Now, folks, listen up. I was terrified. Plenty terrified. Heart palpitating. Sweat dripping off my brow. And hands shaking. My survival training kicked in. I sat down, swigged three or four gulps of water from my canteen. Took deep breaths. And calm returned. I rose and hugged Mister Chu and mumbled something like, "Thank you. I'm in your debt." I got our caravan moving, and we arrived at the place where we were supposed to be.

SIX

USS Panay, Yangtze River, Shanghai, China, June 1937

By mid-1937 I was ready for my next assignment. The intelligence office on Admiral Yarnell's staff, Commander Asiatic Fleet, recommended that my next assignment be with ship's company on the gunboat *USS Panay** (107) as Chief Radioman. Currently, she was anchored in the Yangtze off the Bund (the International Settlement) in Shanghai. Admiral Yarnell concurred.

In a private conversation, the Admiral tasked me with a secret assignment that only he, his staff intelligence officer, and I knew about it. I reckon nowadays I can tell you about it. Naval intelligence was desperate to know about the Imperial Japanese Navy's preparations for the upcoming Pacific War against the Occidental colonialist powers in the Orient. My confidential task was to intercept Japanese maritime traffic, translate it, and pass it to a cut-out in Shanghai.

I reported aboard the *USS Panay* on 16 June 1937. The skipper, Lieutenant Commander James Hughes, tasked me with organizing the radio room, fixing and tuning the equipment, and getting it operating at one-hundred percent. Wow, what a mess! The shack was, how should I say, a stinking disaster. Most of the equipment was marginally functional, some not at all. My assistant, Radioman Third Class James Murphy, and I held a vigorous field day. At the end of that day, the shack shone. Next, Murphy and I tackled the equipment. That took considerably longer. We ordered vacuum tubes and all manner of stuff from fleet stores. Fortunately, the Asiatic fleet supply ship was anchored in Shanghai. Repairs proceeded apace. Within a few days, message traffic was flowing routinely. One afternoon the skipper entered my shack, looked about, and said, "Chief Marne, I'm impressed."

I reckon the skipper knew that I had a covert intelligence assignment that he was not privy. As long as I kept the message traffic flowing correctly and promptly, he left me alone.

The Panay's company was assigned to one of four duty sections. Every fourth day, the duty section was restricted to the ship and the company stood the watches. Because of my duties, I was not in a duty section; instead, I stood watch-stander's duty; that is, I manned the radio shack when required. Other times, I worked on my "other" assignment. Once in a while, my tasks diminished and I could leave the ship, at liberty to do what I wanted. I limited my wanderings to the International Settlement— the Bund area.* (108) Actually, with my SCI clearance, I was warned not to enter the Chinese section of the city. Nonetheless, I exercised caution on such times ashore. I was aware of my surroundings and was prudent in my activities. Usually, I went on liberty dressed in one of my custom-made suits from Hong Kong. Earlier I mentioned my "cut out." My contact was a petroleum engineer with the Standard Oil Socony Vacuum Company in Shanghai. In "real life" she was a senior agent with the State Department's Bureau of Research and Intelligence.* (109)

I knew this person as Amanda Muñoz. Not her real name, I reckon, but *C'est la vie*. She was about thirty years old, comely, and tall for a woman, with dark brown eyes, jet black hair, and an easy smile. She carried a few extra pounds, and claimed to be from Taos, New Mexico. I sort'a believed her because, when I listened closely, I could detect a faint Spanish accent in her voice.

I'd schedule a meeting with her when I had important Japanese message traffic of interest to the Executive Department, or timely maritime messages from "others." Oftentimes we met in a small White Russian tea house in a nondescript alley off the Bund.* I went ashore in mufti, sometimes dressed as a tourist, other times as a businessman, and sometimes as "who knows what."

Note: Thank you, U.S. Navy, for my spiffy tailor-made ensemble,

Hong Kong's finest.* (110)

Our meetings were short and professional. She'd sip her tea and I would drink my coffee, occasionally with a touch of Kentucky's finest. I would slip her the relevant traffic in the folds of the English-language newspaper, *The Central China Chronicle,* or a restaurant menu, or whatever. And she'd insert it in her wide portfolio. It was not that sophisticated a ploy, but it seemed to work well enough.

That slight bulge in her dress by her left calf was telling—the lady was armed. She projected a mien that signaled she knew how to use that weapon with professional acumen. I did not know the make, model, or caliber, but I reckoned that her *pistola* was one of those lady's 32s. My 1911 Colt 45, in a thin holster, was concealed in the folds of my custom-tailored suit jacket.

Please understand that Shanghai was flooded with foreign agents: Japanese, British, Chinese, French, German, Soviets, and freelance operatives from just about any place one could imagine. Would you believe the Vatican? If we were turned, I did not know it, and Mistress Muñoz did not comment. In fact, she never said much. Nevertheless, no one bothered us that I could tell.

More about Amanda Muñoz later.

As a United States gunboat on patrol on the Yangtze, we tackled a potpourri of assignments: Naval infantry sorties on bandit suppression missions; warlord counter insurgencies; rescuing American and Occidental missionaries, businessmen, and diplomatic personnel; escorting Occidental shipping with fire suppression; courier transportation; and most anything to protect American and other Occidental interests. From time to time, some of my shipmates were wounded—a couple seriously. Pharmacist Mate First Class James Steel treated and dressed wounds, applied splints, and dispensed appropriate nostrums. We promptly got the seriously wounded to St. Elizabeth's Presbyterian Hospital in Shanghai; those with lesser wounds would recover in our Sick Bay. Other times, when we could not engage the miscreants directly, we innovated. Don't ask how. That's the *Panay's* secret.

I'll summarize one of our sorties that exemplifies a key element of our responsibilities. Early morning on 15 October 1937, *HMS Ladybird,**

(111) a British gunboat on the Yangtze, sent us a FLASH message *en clair* requesting assistance. The radio operator at the British Petroleum terminal at Wuhu had sent a Morse code signal to the British consulate in Shanghai detailing the Warlord General Lu Jung-t'ing's* (112) raid and looting of the Episcopal mission at Liuchow—about twenty miles north of Wuhu. A young girl at the mission had hidden in a well and escaped that night. She told the details to British company officials at the terminal.

The general's men had gang-raped the female Chinese converts and then murdered all the Chinese at the mission: men, women, and children—some by the abhorrent death of a thousand cuts and some of the men by agonizing crucifixion. Before the mass executions, General Lu harangued the Chinese Christian converts for their abandonment of their culture's traditional Buddhist religion and for adopting the Occidental's false Christian religion. General Lu Jung-t'ing held the minister, his wife, and their three girl children hostage, and demanded 100,000 British pounds sterling for their ransom.

We joined *Ladybird* about ten miles north of Wuhu. Lieutenant Commander Charmodly Smyth Worthington, Commanding Officer of the *HMS Ladybird,* was the senior officer present. He formed a combined naval infantry company and advanced to the mission. Because of my Top Secret code-word clearance and requirement to man the *Panay's* radio, I was forbidden to join the naval infantry company. Onboard, I stood watch packing my 1911 Colt 45—enough of a kick to keep miscreants at bay or in an underground suite.

During the firefight, our Browning automatic 30-caliber rifles* (113) and Thompson 45-caliber* (114) submachine guns cut down the warlord mercenaries in droves. We had two men wounded slightly. Unfortunately, just as capture was imminent, the warlord general Lu murdered his hostages. Outraged, Lieutenant Commander Smyth Worthington captured General Lu Jung-t'ing, took him aboard the *Ladybird,* and hung him from the main mast. His rationalization was "the law of the sea," and he tossed the warlord's body into the Yangtze. I didn't realize we were at sea, but *C'est la guerre.*

SEVEN

USS Panay, Yangtze River, Shanghai, China, October 1937

The classified Japanese message traffic was increasing rapidly and the content was more ominous. It was evident to anyone who was awake and over nine years old that the Empire of Japan was soon going to make war on China. (Note: "make war." The Japanese Empire does not declare war and start hostilities. Rather, the Rising Sun strikes with a massive attack on key installations, ignoring international conventions.)

Let's return to Mistress Muñoz. By back channel (don't ask) she communicated that she was now assigned to the Standard Oil Socony Vacuum Geophysical Office in Nanking, and she included her new contact system.

I talked with Lieutenant Commander Hughes and requested that, if feasible, we sail up river to Nanking. Such a move would facilitate my other assignment. I did not tell him why or offer details and, with prudence, he did not ask.

Without ado, he said, "Chief Marne, you're a pain in the ass."

I responded, "Aye, sir. You are correct."

He stared at me askance, rubbed his chin, as was his wont, and said, "Send our movement messages."

Within minutes, I felt the deck vibrate softly as our engines surged to full life.

✳ ✳ ✳ ✳ ✳

In Nanking, Amanda Muñoz and I posed as lovebirds and met in cafes, tea houses, and the like. On greeting her, I'd hug her and kiss her on the cheek. Amanda seemed to enjoy our new charade. In one of our meetings in Oretsky's White Russian Tea House,* (115) during my greeting kiss, she turned her head, kissed me full on the mouth, and pressed her body against mine. Whoops! Not in the playbook. Her coquettish smile extended throughout our meeting, with her *sub rosa* message not so *sub*. I said and did nothing untoward, keeping our relationship professional. She got the message.

Amanda scheduled our next meeting for 16 August, a few days hence, at the Sun Yat-sen restaurant in the Golden Eagle Hotel near the city center. Her reason for this meeting remains unknown. I posed as a businessman from San Francisco representing the United States Pipe Foundry, Inc. I had business cards to substantiate my charade. I dressed in my tan gabardine, three-piece suit, freshly pressed white shirt with faux gold cufflinks in French cuffs, a pale blue tie with thin, dark brown stripes and a real diamond stickpin, and brown wing-tip oxfords.

She was at the table when I entered the restaurant. She extended her right hand; I shook it and presented my card, and we completed our formal introductions. She ordered a Manhattan, I got sweet iced tea with lemon—missed the mint, of course. During lunch we discussed a fictitious pipeline from somewhere to nowhere. Afterward, we made appropriate goodbyes with a schedule to meet again. Great theatre for our audience—whoever that may have been.

❋ ❋ ❋ ❋ ❋

Let's pause. I want to describe the historical record. It's important for you, dear reader, to fully appreciate the developments that will follow.

On 7 July 1937, the Japanese Imperial army staged an attack during their early morning patrol at the Marco Polo Bridge,(116) a few miles northeast of Peiping. The incident was a contrived* casus belli.

Within a few months, the Japanese had captured Peiping, Tsingtao, Mukden, Chefoo, Shanghai, and Canton, and were threatening Nanking, the capital city of the Republic of China. The Nationalist Army fought vigorously but they were out-classed and out-gunned. The Communist Eighth Route Army fought holding actions in northern China, but eventually they had to fall back to their mountain safety havens. The Occidentals were concerned, and their classified messages jammed the airways, or so it seemed.

EIGHT

Nanking, China, September to October 1937

I was walking to the *Panay*. I tripped on a loose stone in the walkway outside the hotel and stripped the heel off my left oxford. Damn! Just what I needed. I was scheduled to be on duty in my radio shack for the second dog watch. I wandered around Hunan Road, the main shopping area, looking for a cobbler shop. After a time, I was about to abandon this search and return to the ship. The machinist mates in the engine room could reattach the heel, though in what condition, I could not imagine.

Soon, I spotted this narrow alley lined with a myriad of shops proffering sundry wares. It was too inviting to skip, so I ambled down the alley. And there it was, a hand-drawn sign that displayed a shoe with a broken heel, hanging over a solid wood door crudely carved with a karst scene. I translated the Chinese glyphs to mean "We fix." Success!

The window display contained inexpensive Chinese art, tourist bric-a-brac, bottles of herbs, and a motley array of mismatched shoes and boots. Tucked in a back corner was a small display of Chinese postage stamps.

As I entered, a small bell attached to the inside of the door tinkled softly. In contrast to the window, the shop was spick-and-span clean, well lit, and with merchandise arranged neatly on waist-high tables. Against the south wall, the more delicate pieces were displayed on metal racks. The aisles were wide enough to move about easily. Amazing! Most shops of this ilk were jammed with bric-a-brac and tourist junk randomly scattered on display tables jammed side by side, leaving marginal room to move. In the background I heard the hum of light machinery—the shoe repair apparatus, I reckoned.

The proprietress emerged softly from behind a dark-blue beaded curtain at the back of the shop. She was petite, and strikingly beautiful. She had large, dark brown, playful eyes, a wide mouth with full lips, and bright olive skin. Her precisely combed, long, black hair cascaded over her shoulders, and her curves strained at the silk in her powder blue, gold-rib-trimmed sham fu.

I was taken aback and stood awkwardly, slightly inside the door. I had seen many beautiful Chinese women—none as lovely as she. I reckoned that her age was somewhere between eighteen and twenty years.

She moved gracefully toward me and with a winsome, slow smile, spoke softly. "Welcome to my humble shop, mister Occidental gentleman. How may I be of service?"

Delightful. Her English had a tinge of the British, indicating she probably had been educated at an Anglican mission. She noticed my limp, and spotted my shoe with the missing heel. "My father is the cobbler." She led me to a small, well-appointed room, and indicated a rosewood chair covered in medium-blue brocade. After a signal that I did not see, a female servant entered and placed a tea service and a plate of biscuits on the rosewood and teak table. A small stream of vapors curled upward from the teapot. "Permit me to pour," she said.

Proper, charming, and classic Oriental hospitality. I enjoyed the tea and biscuits, but mostly I enjoyed looking at and chatting with this enchanting Oriental woman.

"Please remove your shoe. I will take it to the back." In a minute or two she returned and handed me a handwritten receipt in Chinese glyphs. "Please remain. Your shoe will be ready quickly."

I read the message on the ticket and tucked it into my vest pocket. I smiled at her and said, "Your price is fair."

Her eyes widened in curious surprise. "Excuse me, sir. You read Mandarin?"

I had goofed. It was imprudent for me to display my language skills, such as they were. "I collect Chinese stamps, and I know a few glyphs," I lied. I know nothing about Chinese philately, but that's the excuse that popped into my head. Must have been that stamp display in the window that triggered my response.

With that intriguing, slow smile, she commented, "Dear sir, I am impressed that you would respect the Middle Kingdom by collecting our postage stamps and learning to read Mandarin glyphs." She stood and extended her right hand to me. "Permit me to introduce myself. I am Veronica Chong. My widowed father, Chong Sung-ling, and I are privileged to have this emporium. As you see, we offer for sale a menagerie of merchandise. However, it is our shoe trade that maintains this business." She blushed slightly and continued. "I realize that it is imprudent for me to speak so forthrightly to a stranger—especially an Occidental. But, I am a modern woman, and I've outgrown most of the operatic conventions that have stultified our society's interpersonal communication. Please tell me who you are, if you would be so kind."

Whoops! Her candid barrage overwhelmed my comprehension. It took two or three seconds for me to compose myself and respond with coherence. "Good afternoon, Mistress Chong, I'm delighted to meet you." I shook her hand, and said, "My name is Matthew Marne." I paused to consider if I should continue the lie of my meeting with Amanda. Instead, I chose, "I am a sailor in the United States Navy, and I operate the radios on that gunboat in the Yangtze—the *United States Ship Panay.*"

A slow frown crept across Veronica's forehead. Her eyes narrowed and her head held straight. She placed her arms akimbo, and increased the spread of her feet; her hands curled into fists—the confrontation stance. She said nothing as her mind whirled.

Did I goof, again? Clearly, my truth disturbed Veronica, a Chinese citizen. Had she categorized me as one of our rowdy sailors on liberty: drunk, boisterous, and carousing with *filles de joies?* I could almost see the images flashing in her mind: Occidental imperialism, alien gunboats on our rivers, unequal treaties, occupation of key port city, opium to enslave the people, and foreign laws for foreigners.

She began to relax. "Mister Marne, your attire belies your occupation. You project the image of a successful businessman; your three-piece ensemble is *haute*, your speech is cultured, and your manners are gallant. Yet, your regular costume is the uniform of a sailor in the United States Navy. I am confused."

"I understand, Mistress Chong. Permit me to explain. Several months ago, I had a seven-day leave. I flew to Hong Kong on China National Airlines. Walked about the island seeing the sights and absorbing the culture of this British Crown Colony." I added quickly, "Now British because of the unjust opium wars and unequal treaties." I sipped tea and continued, "Because Hong Kong is known for its fine tailoring at attractive prices, I purchased several items of tailor-made clothing, including this suit and my oxfords."

Mistress Chong eased her stance and offered a small smile. "I see, Mister Marne. I appreciate your understanding of the unjust British wars to flood China with Indian opium."

That's better. I'm mending fences, as it were. "Yesterday, an acquaintance of mine, a radio operator in the United States Embassy, suggested that I meet a female engineer in his office. Accordingly, I dressed to impress the lady. This noon, we had lunch at the Golden Eagle Hotel. I was returning to the *Panay* when my heel broke. And here I am." Damn, lying was becoming far too easy.

The frown returned. "You have positive feelings for this female acquaintance?"

Her question was imprudent, but it indicated that Veronica had interest. "She was nice, comely, and most professional. I doubt that I shall contact her in the future."

That slow smile returned. "Please call me 'Veronica' and I shall call you 'Matthew.' If you do not object."

"I shall be most pleased."

Her father entered and handed me the professionally repaired oxford. He had a pronounced limp and used a cane—carved ebony, I suspected. He was a small, husky fellow about sixty years old. Veronica made the introduction. He spent a few seconds examining me intently and then quizzed Veronica. He spoke rapidly in Mandarin and with an accent that made his speech difficult to understand. I recognized a few words now and then, but did not get the gist of their conversation.

"My father is flattered that an Occidental of your obvious stature has visited his inadequate shop. He wishes to know about you. My apologies, Mister Marne, it is improper for me to ask personal questions. To please my father, however, be so kind to tell us some relevant details of your life experiences: parents, home, marriage, education, naval career, and so forth."

Curious. Why the in-depth questioning the first time here? *¿Quién sabe?* "I am pleased to share some of my experiences with you and your father. First, I am not married and never have been." With that key fact established, I told Veronica about my early life, my Navy experience, heavily edited, of course, and my goal upon retirement of earning that electrical engineering degree.

Chong listened intently to my rhetoric. I suspect that he had enough skill in English to follow my oral biography. His body motion was positive as his daughter relayed my life story. Once in a while, he would look at me and nod his head; at other times he would smile. At the end of the story, he clasped my right hand and shook it vigorously. He began speaking in Mandarin faster than I could understand. Veronica relayed his story in the King's English.

The highlight of Mister Chong's life story began in the late 1890s. As a young man of twenty-three, he worked as a cook's assistant in the U.S. Marines' barracks in Peking. In 1899, the Chinese ultranationalist organization *Yiheguan (The Righteous and Harmonious Fists),* a movement dubbed the 'Boxers'* (117) for the members' martial skills, began its terror campaign in China's Shandong Province. Their goal was to expel the 'white devils' that were despoiling the Celestial Empire with Occidental culture, religion, and opium. The Boxers massacred Christian missionaries, Chinese Christians, and Occidental civilians, destroying churches, railroad stations, and Occidental-owned property. On 20 June 1900, the Boxers and the Qing Empire's Imperial Army began a siege of the Occidental section of Peking—location of the international legations, businesses, and schools. This area was surrounded by the Tartar Wall,* (118) an ancient stone wall some forty-five feet tall.

Sir Claude MacDonald* (119) formed a battalion of international troops to man the Tartar Wall and defend the Legation area.* (120) The fighting was intense and the Chinese suffered severe casualties. Several days into the siege, a United States Marine corporal fell with a bullet in his chest. At the time, Chong was on the wall bringing food and water to the Marines. He retrieved the corporal's rifle, took the Marine's position on the wall, and began firing, with surprising accuracy—he dropped several Boxers and a Chinese army officer. That afternoon, the Qing army placed two ancient, muzzle-loaded cannons several hundred meters from the wall.* (121)

The bombardment of the Tartar Wall began. It was not particularly effective but it was harassing. Late that afternoon, a ball exploded near Chang. He took shrapnel in his right thigh and shoulder, and shards cut several deep gashes into his back. Seriously wounded, he lay bleeding from a severed artery in his leg. A Marine private left his post to fetch a Navy corpsman. The fellow reached Chong, applied a tourniquet above the leg wound, swabbed the wounds with a dilute iodine solution, applied compresses to the other wounds to stop the bleeding, and washed his entire body with Dakin solution—a potent disinfectant.

Captain John T. Myers, USMC,* (122) Officer in Charge of the Marine contingent, overruled the Navy surgeon's objection to operating on a Chinaman. Within the hour, Chong was on the operating table in the dispensary. He spent most of the siege in sickbay recovering slowly and surely.

An international military force landed at Tientsin and fought Chinese Imperial troops en route to Peking. After 55 days of the siege, on 14 August 1900, the international army fought into central Peking and soundly defeated the Imperial army and the Boxers. The relief force occupied Peking, and the Dowager Empress, Tz'u-his,* (123) and her staff fled the capitol in disguise.

Captain Myers ordered his Marine detachment in formation. In a formal ceremony, Meyers issued a certificate to Chong Sung-ling that affirmed he was an honorary United States Marine with the rank of corporal. The Captain placed a campaign hat, complete with the Marines' metal emblem, on Chong's head.* (124) "Corporal Chong, your steadfast courage on the Tartar wall in defense of the International Legation, Peking, was exemplary and brought honor to you, your family, and your country. I shall personally ensure that your name is entered into the rolls of the United States Marine Corps in Washington, D.C."

Chong stood stiffly at attention and saluted Captain Meyers. "You honor me more than I deserve," he said. He executed the about-face maneuver expertly and, using his Navy-issued cane, marched out of the International Settlement, Peking. If someone had looked carefully, they'd have spotted a tear on Chong's cheeks.

"That's an amazing story of true courage. Mister Chong, I must say that your induction into the U.S. Marine Corps for your resolutely brave action on the Tartar Wall is well deserved. May I offer my congratulations."

Chong nodded his head vigorously and smiled.

Veronica had a curious expression. "Matthew, this is the first time I have heard the complete story regarding my father's U.S. Marine hat. He must have developed a special affinity for you."

Meantime, Chong had left the room. He returned in a short minute. In his right hand was that Marine campaign hat.* With his sleeve, he polished the Marine emblem, and with a short bow, he offered the hat to me. "You see."

I handled the hat gingerly, looked at all sides, and gazed at the emblem for a few seconds. Handing the hat back to Mister Chong, I said, "I am impressed with your award. I see that you treasure it with great affection. I understand." Veronica translated.

"Yes, mister sailor. Much treasure. I am a United States Marine Corporal, honorary."

Mister Chong had spoken in English, somewhat broken, but I followed it.

He rose to leave, spoke to Veronica, shook my hand vigorously, and looked me in the eyes. "You come back see me. Now, have happy time with

Veronica." Then he spoke rapidly to Veronica in a dialect I did not know.

I rose as he left the room. Shortly, the subtle sound of the machinery operating suffused through the room.

"May I ask what your father said?"

She blushed slightly and refilled our cups. "Please have another biscuit. They are tasty, not so?"

"Yes. Indeed, the biscuits are delicious."

After the ceremony of tea pouring and sipping, Veronica brushed away an imaginary crumb. She looked at me with her soft smile and spoke in a courteous voice. "My father sees you as an honorable young man, and was impressed that you are a Chinese philatelist. When you return, if you would be pleased, he will show you his inventory of special Chinese postage stamps."

"Tell your father that I appreciate his offer, and I am looking forward to reviewing his Chinese stamps." Damn! I was getting deeper and deeper in this charade. To what end?

"Also, he wanted me to tell you of his great affection for your country—the United States of America. He commented that the Americans are the one country of Occidentals that have empathy with the Chinese people. They provide diplomatic support and on-scene assistance with their treasures and blood. And they seek nothing in return. What a great country."

I looked at my watch and saw time a' flying. "Veronica, I must leave, else I'll be late for my watch." Not having courted an Oriental woman before, I was unsure how to proceed. This intriguing woman had enchanted me. With my courage at full measure, I said, "I am delighted to have met you and your wonderful father. With your permission, I will visit you again shortly."

She offered her biggest smile, and took my right hand and pressed it to her cheek. "Indeed, I shall be honored for you to return to my shop to see me. I will have a singular tea for you."

I was smitten with Veronica.

NINE

USS Panay, Yangtze, Nanking, China, November to December 1937

The message traffic had increased significantly—Japanese, British, French, Italian, Dutch, Portuguese, even Siamese. And, of course, U.S. Japanese troop movement messages flooded my IN basket. The Japanese attack on Nanking was imminent.

In the following week, I visited Veronica and her father at every opportunity. In a visit in late November, Chong showed me the gems of his Chinese stamps. "Please view with pleasure."

His collection or stock, I don't know which, was in a delicately carved teak box. Each of his stamps was in a glassine envelope. To keep the stamp from being bent, every envelope had a thin, black, plastic backing cut to the exact size of the envelope. Chong selected one of the stamps. He used stamp teasers with flat tips to remove it from its envelope, and he placed it on a small, black silk square. "I got this unused 5¢, 1878, dark-yellow and green dragon from a mandarin in Shandong Province." From the folds of his gown, he withdrew a two-power magnifying glass and handed it to me. "Use this lens to see well. Notice the dragon stamp's extremely fine condition—free from flaws."

I had no clue what I was looking at. Nonetheless, I uttered, "Very nice."

Next he displayed an array of four red stamps. "These unused 1897, large, 3¢ surcharge on the red revenue stamps, came to me from a nondescript fellow representing an anonymous mogul in Shanghai. Seems that he had troubles with the British constabulary in the International Zone for peddling Indian opium to madams of brothels and masters of opium dens." Chong's display of Chinese stamps continued apace for about thirty minutes. I had no knowledge or appreciation of Chong's running display of Chinese stamps. Nonetheless, I was impressed. Not by what I saw and heard, but by Chong's knowledge and enthusiasm for his obviously rare and valuable Chinese stamp collection.

"One more stamp to see, Mister Matthew." He opened a small rosewood box, withdrew the glassine envelope, and with delicate care removed the stamp, placing it on the silk. A wide smile crept across his face. "This is the gem of my collection. Notice the vivid red color of this stamp."

I had no cogent response; nevertheless, I uttered, "Indeed, its color is more intense than on the other red stamps."

"Yes. It is so." Chong continued with an eager voice, "This the 1897, 4¢ small surcharge on the 3¢ red revenue.* (125) This is the finest copy of the few known to exist. Please notice that this red revenue stamp has not been used." With his flat-tipped tweezers, he turned the stamp face down. "See that the gum is evenly distributed and not disturbed." He turned the stamp face up. "This red revenue is superbly well centered, the perforations are complete and not bent. It truly is a gem." He looked at me to get my reaction and, I reckon, my approval.

"Mister Chong, I see your pride of ownership of this beautiful and rare red revenue stamp. I congratulate you."

Chong bowed deeply, and offered, "It is best that I do not speak of my acquisition of this stamp. It would be imprudent for me to discuss the provenance of this 4¢ small surcharge." He pointed his left hand towards the back of the shop. "Today, I showed you the samples. Many more Chinese stamps in my vault."

A few days later, after my meeting with mistress Muñoz, I headed for the British Embassy. I'd heard that they had a large library of technical, historical, and general knowledge books. Sure enough, with the help of the lady librarian, I was soon perusing the 1936 edition of Stanley Gibbons Worldwide Stamp Catalogue, its China section. Whoops! Several blinks later, I worked to resolve my astonishment. The price for that small piece of red paper, the 4¢ small surcharge, was beyond reason. Mind you, that price number was in pounds sterling, not U.S.A. dollars.

TEN

Nanking, China, November and early December 1937

'll summarize. An ominous ambiance pervaded the Chinese scene in Nanking. The message traffic reported the Japanese Army conquest of China's port cities as they advanced down the east coast. The Japanese aggression suggested that in a year or two, they would war with the United States and the European colonial powers.

I spent all my spare time with Veronica. Regrettably, she was consumed with her responsibility to her shop. Tea and biscuits prevailed. Occasionally, we would go to a venue of some sort to view a motion picture—sometimes Chinese, other times a British or American picture. Once in a while we visited the His Wu Lake Park.* (126) I reckon it mattered not where we were. We were together.

Veronica and I were an item, not in the gossip section of the British newspaper or the Nanking Times, but in our hearts. We fell in love, deeply in love.

We were at the park watching the swans do what swans do. The sky was overcast and it was chilly. Our conversation was desultory as we knew that soon I'd be shipping out and the Japanese Kwangtung Army would conquer Nanking.

There was a long pause in our badinage. Veronica looked at me with her slow smile. She took my hand and broke the silence with a soft voice. "Matthew, my love, I wish that we would be married." She wrapped her arms around me and kissed me deeply. (May I say, passionately?)

I must say that her proposal was unexpected. Naturally, I was thrilled and desired to have Veronica for my wife. But to what end? "Veronica, I love you dearly." I paused slightly to prepare my response. "As much as I want you for my wife, our marriage is impossible in these troubled times."

The Navy forbad its members from marrying Oriental women—from marrying at all, for that matter. And I had a most serious commitment to Uncle Sam's Navy that I could not abrogate. If I were to marry Veronica, I'd be arrested *post haste*. The members of the General Court Marshal would convict me on the first ballot, and my special intelligence clearances would be revoked. I'd spend the next few years of my life in the Leavenworth Military Prison.

I suspect that Veronica knew that I could not marry her. She was bright, and well informed. Nonetheless, she made the marriage proposition to express her love, and with the hope I would accept.

Veronica devised a compromise. "Matthew, I know in my heart that we cannot marry. My father and I offer to make our apartment over the shop your home ashore." She blushed slightly. "And to please share my bed."

A tempting offer that racked my soul. I could not do it. Not without a marriage license and a proper religious ceremony. "My love, we will marry after the war and raise our children honorably, away from the chaos that pervades the Orient."

Tears flowed down her cheeks. She smiled tentatively. "Yes. That is what we will do."

I suspect that in her heart she knew that destiny would capture our dreams.

Chong reluctantly accepted that Veronica and I would not marry now. He knew that the Japanese conquest of Nanking was only a few weeks away. "Mister Marne, perhaps you would consider a Chinese ceremony. I will be your sponsor. It would be a glorious day. All our friends in this place will help prepare and attend with best wishes. There will be a colorful dragon parade with Veronica in the sedan and costumed in traditional Chinese dress, drums and gongs to scare away evil thoughts, firecrackers, and acrobats." He smiled widely. "Permit me to make the announcement."

"Mister Chong, your thoughtful and heartfelt proposal tempts me intensely. Most regretfully, I may not accept. Please understand that the Navy's orders constrain my activities. I am forbidden to marry."

The light faded from his eyes. "You are to be my son, one day soon, I pray."

Veronica and I spent as much time together as was possible—celibately, of course. No more about that.

In early December, the war clouds over Nanking darkened sharply, and it was apparent that I'd be leaving shortly.

Chong realized that within a few days the Kwangtung Army of the Empire of Japan would capture Nanking and take or destroy everything and everyone Chinese, an inferior race in Japanese eyes. He implored me to take his special collection of valuable Chinese stamps and return them after the war. I protested with regret that I could not accept that responsibility. What was I to do with this philatelic treasure? "Mister Chong, we'll be in a war in a few days, I have no place to protect them, and I do not know my future circumstances. I cannot accept your valuable Chinese stamps."

"I beg you, Mister Matthew, take my collection. I cannot envision the Japanese destroying these treasures when they know nothing of them. Please take them away from Nanking."

I was in an untenable position. "My dear friend, Corporal Chung of the United States Marines, I am unable to take your Chinese stamps. I cannot protect them. I do not know what to do with them. As much as I want to help you, I am unable. Please understand."

Near tears, he renewed his appeal—this time with an Oriental gambit. "I give you my collection of Chinese stamps. They are yours. Keep them. I'll renounce ownership in a formal Bill of Sale notarized by an officer at the American Embassy. After the war, sell them and use the funds to begin a new life with Veronica."

Whoops! That was a kicker. He had boxed me into a no-win scenario. If I refused, I would be renouncing Veronica. If I accepted, I'd be committed to a responsibility to Veronica that might not be appropriate in a few years. I could not envision this coming war—its disruption, its military and civilian casualties, its destruction and chaos, its after-effects. What would be the nature of the world after the peace? Clever, clever was Mister Chong. With a touch of miff, I said, "Mister Chong, you have foxed me into accepting your collection."

With a broad grin of success, he replied, "I knew in my heart you would take my stamps. Thank you." From under the table he removed a leather portfolio. All the edges were sealed in wax and the wax at the lock was impressed with the Marine emblem. "The gems are here and there are many other valuable stamps and covers. I am confident that you will manage successfully." He handed me the key on a ring. "Inside the folio is the Bill of Sale. To conclude legally this sale, you must give me one dollar in American currency."

Defeated totally, I admired Chong's intricate ploy and his deft execution. He was right, of course. I had to have a legal document that confirmed the sale of these Chinese treasures. I put a silver dollar in his left hand, and shook his right hand. "We have a deal, Mister Chong." I tucked the valise under my arm. "Thank you, Mister Chong. I will do my best to safeguard these Chinese stamps." In an hour, I had to stand a watch aboard the *Panay*. I took the portfolio by the handle. "Veronica, it is time to leave, I'm due aboard ship. I'll see you tomorrow." I embraced my love and kissed her. "I love you dearly." We held our embrace far too long.

I hailed a rickshaw on Hunan Road and headed toward the Yangtze. Rolling, I missed the scenes of this beautiful city. Images of Veronica, her father, and Chinese philately pervaded my mind. How could I help Veronica and Chong escape this city? What was I to do with these philatelic treasures? Had to get them to a safe place and out of Nanking before the Japanese entered. What were my options? Store them on the *Panay*? Out of the question. Total nonsense. Mail them via the Chinese postal system to the American Embassy in Hankow? Seriously a dumb idea. Ship them via American Express to the folks in Marfa? Too late. The Japanese would intercept all transportation out of Nanking. The conundrum was perplexing, and I had no solution. I pushed my mind to find an unorthodox answer.

We arrived at the *Panay's* gangway. I was about to exit the rickshaw when the light atop my head burst on brightly. Using Mandarin with muddled tones, I told the runner to head for the United States Embassy on Hunan Road. It was risky, but it was the only option I had at this late date.

I entered the abandoned intelligence spaces and spotted Chief Petty Officer Joshua Abrams. He was petty officer in charge of the special access intelligence vault. Just the person I needed. Joshua was a tall, lanky fellow from Casper, Wyoming. Actually, he was from a horse ranch about twenty miles from the city. His wife and two children lived with his parents on the ranch.

Josh was wearing the tropical white uniform with pith helmet, and he had on leggings and a guard belt that carried a holstered 1911 Colt 45. Those accessories on his uniform meant he was naval infantry and was prepared for trouble.

He spoke first. "What the Hell are you doing here, Marne, you asshole?"

"Josh, you wound my soul. Are we not buddies? Have we not toasted Jean Harlow with Kentucky's finest? Have I not befriended you when the fruit of the vine overcame you in the finest bistros in this beautiful city? Do we not share our countries' intelligence secrets?"

Joshua scrunched his face and spit out, "Ya. Ya. Etcetera. Etcetera. You stuck me with the bill at our last on-the-town *soirée*. It's twenty-two dollars and change. Pay up, jerk."

Whoops! He was correct. "Josh, my error, I apologize." Within seconds, I'd taken $25 from my wallet and handed it to him. "We're even. Keep the change."

Mollified, he snapped, "What are you doin' here?"

"A favor. A simple favor from you, ol' pal."

"Marne, don't whitewash me with that malarkey. I've no favors left. We're closing shop. The EOD [Explosive Ordinance Disposal] technicians will be here in a few minutes. We going to blow that combination lock to Tokyo. And immediately afterward, I'm shoving off with the intel pouch in that Navy amphibian* (126A) that's waiting for me at our dock and headed for Hankow. And that's the end of the American Embassy in Nanking. The Japs are not going to get any of my 'stuff'."

I'm just in time. "Josh, I need your help. It's important. Please."

"What's so damn important on this last day in Nanking? I'm leaving and have no time to mess with you."

"You taking the SCI pouch with you?"

"Of course, it's the last one."

"Have you sealed it?"

"No. Will do after the vault blows just in case there some stuff remaining."

Pressed for time, he responded with a touch of annoyance. "What's so important about the intel pouch?"

I took the portfolio from under my arm. "Put this portfolio in the pouch. In Hankow, send it to naval intelligence headquarters through our secure system. Send a back channel message to Chief Tony Belli alerting him that my portfolio is en route and to hold it for Chief Radioman Matthew Marne, USN. I'll retrieve it, sometime in the future."

"Marne, you are out of your idiot mind. I'm retiring in a few months, and I'm not going to jeopardize it and spend time in Leavenworth for doing you an illegal favor. End of message. That's 'thirty.' *Comprenez vous?*"

His curiosity surged. "What's in that leather whatever?"

"It's not cash, or drugs, or jewelry, or anything ill-gotten. It legal and very valuable, and I'm its custodian. I'm not privileged to say more."

"Can't do it. Shove off, ol' pal. See you in the next war."

"Let's see, Josh. I can't recall. What *was* her name? Lovely female. You must remember her? She's the one with the oversized bosoms that struggled to burst out of her low-cut blouse, long blond hair, and those very long legs she proudly displayed. Very nice, indeed." I paused to get Josh's reaction. His eyes were beginning to narrow and his hand tightened on the pouch's leather strap. "I got it! It's Hilda. That's her name. It's Hildegard. She was the code clerk at the German Embassy. As I recall, ol' pal, you fraternized with her from time to time. Not so?"

With venom, he spit, "Marne, I always knew you were a flaming asshole. Give me that damn portfolio and I'll take care of it. You have my word."

"Many thanks, Chief Abrams." I grabbed his hand and shook it vigorously; on impulse, I stood on my toes and kissed his right cheek. Before he could respond, I executed an about-face and scooted away. As I was about to exit the intelligence spaces, his booming voice called out, "Asshole."

I was walking to the *Panay,* and my mind was awhirl with issues. The explosion was muffled, but I heard it, perhaps because I was expecting it. Aboard ship, my assistant James Murphy said, "It's been busy." He showed me the stack of traffic that I needed to work.

It was catharsis, actually. Got my mind off civilian issues. After midnight, lying in my bunk, I decided that after the war, if I survived, I would go back to Nanking and return the stamps to Chong or to Veronica. By then, who knew what our relationship would be, if any.

ELEVEN

Nanking, Chong's shop, early December

"Mister Chong, you and Veronica must escape the city. Go to relatives or friends in the country where you will be safe. It's prudent to go now."

Veronica came to me, hugged and kissed me with intense passion, then began to sob. She knew her fate. I could not imagine it.

Chong responded, now in more articulate English. "We have no one to visit. All our relatives have died of disease, or were tragically murdered by bandits or warlords. And the news in the alley is that the roads out of Nanking are choked with Chinese troops marching into the city and they have established military roadblocks. Already the Yangtze is crowded with junks sailing up river. We are stuck in Nanking."

Stunned, I stood silently. The reality of Chong's comments ripped at my soul. "Surely, there is some way to protect you and Veronica."

He dropped his eyes. "Mister Matthew, perhaps there is one way to spirit Veronica out of the city. I would ask that you take Veronica aboard the *Panay* as a stowaway."

I shook my head at this outrageous suggestion. Nonetheless, I would have been tempted if there had been a reasonable chance of success. "Marine Corporal Chong, your idea is inventive. But it is impossible. Every inch of that ship is occupied. Veronica would be found within minutes, returned to shore, handed to the Chinese police and jailed—a horrible outcome not to be considered. I would be arrested and go to prison."

Chong responded soulfully, "Yes. You are correct, stowaway is not workable. I have no more options."

Veronica, slightly recovered, poured tea and served the indomitable biscuits. She sat close to me and I felt her love. Silence suffused throughout the room. On impulse, I commented, "Disguise Veronica as a boy. That ploy might give her some refuge from the Japanese."

Chong looked at me with incredulous eyes, then glanced at Veronica. "She could never pass as a boy."

Note: The Imperial Japanese Kwangtung Army entered Nanking 12 December 1937.* (127) What followed was the "Rape of Nanking"—one of the most egregious atrocities of World War II.* (128)

My heart cries. I cannot continue with this scenario. Maybe later. For now, let's return to the main elements of this narrative, aboard the *USS Panay*.

TWELVE

USS Panay, Yangtze River, en route to Wuhu, China,
Sunday, 12 December,1937

The trip up the Yangtze was routine. Those not on duty were lounging, enjoying the day. At 0830 hours, when we were about seven miles south of Wuhu, Japanese Reserve Colonel of Artillery Kingoro Hahimoto* (129) ordered the thirteenth Heavy Field Battery to open fire on the *Panay*'s convoy. The skipper called General Quarters. The forward and aft gun crews loaded rounds into our two three-inch, fifty-caliber rifles, slammed the breeches locked, swung them toward the Japanese batteries, and were ready for counter battery fire. For reasons I do not understand, Lieutenant Commander Hughes did not give the order to fire. We were under attack for about five minutes. Fortunately, no artillery shells hit the *Panay*. However, splashes spewed shrapnel amongst the convoy and several hit my ship—we suffered no casualties.

The *HMS Ladybird,* anchored near the northeast bank, took six hits—killing one rating and wounding four, two seriously. Several of the junks were hit and two sank with all hands. At 0940 hours, we were several miles from our anchorage. A Japanese patrol boat hailed the *Panay* and commanded us to heave to and prepare to receive an Imperial Japanese Army officer. On orders from Captain Hughes, our engineering officer, Lieutenant Clark Geist, cut power to the ship's triple expansion steam engines. Under the directions of Boatswain Mate First Class Homer Truax, the special sea and anchor detail dropped anchor about midstream. The OOD (Officer of the Deck), Ensign Dennis Biwerse, and the skipper went to quarter deck to receive the Japanese officer. A Japanese Army captain and a squad of his armed naval infantry boarded our ship. I noticed that the officer did not render honors to our flag on the aft gaff or to the OOD at the head of the accommodations ladder. Ensign Biwerse did salute the senior Japanese captain as he stepped onto the quarterdeck. His naval infantry surrounded the quarterdeck and put their rifles at port arms.

Gunner's Mate Second Class John N. Hennessy, seeing the potential for disaster, rousted his gang, opened the armory, and armed his men with Thompson submachine guns and Browning automatic rifles. Without notice, he deployed his men in positions to optimize their field of fire should the Japanese make trouble.

The Japanese officer, in an authoritative and condescending English accent, queried Captain Hughes: "Why did you leave your anchorage at Nanking? Where are you bound? How many civilians are onboard? Who are they?" And a number of other none of his business questions.

The skipper answered his first two or three questions and then responded, "Respectfully, I choose not answer any more of your questions. This conference is concluded."

Affronted by the white man's disrespect, the Japanese officer looked about and saw the motley conglomeration of passengers, including the Chinese citizens and the newsreel cameramen taking motion pictures of the scene. He gave the order, "Captain, you may proceed." Without additional comment, he and his men debarked, again without proper honors. Their patrol boat sped downriver. During his time onboard, the Japanese officer made no mention of any danger ahead. We weighed anchor and got underway. The other ships and junks followed us in trail.

At about 1100 hours, we were anchored in mid-river near Hoshien. The sky was clear and sunny, and the river was flowing quietly. It was Sunday and seventy-five percent of ship's company were in the stand-down mode. I was standing watch in the radio shack.

The *Panay* displayed the American flags as on the day before. The senior consular officer onboard, Mister George Atchison, gave me a position-message to send to our makeshift Embassy in Hankow. I copied

Commander Asiatic Fleet, and our consular office in Peiping, now under Japanese occupation. As a matter of routine, I copied all movement and position messages to the staff of the Japanese Army Commander, Prince Yasuhiko Asaka Yasihiko—the senior officer in the Nanking area.* (130)

Shortly after, I sent our position message to the British shipping in the Yangtze, and to several other addressees in my 'green door' community.

THIRTEEN

*USS Panay, Yangtze River, en route to Wuhu, China,
Sunday, 12 December 1937*

At 1335 hours, the forward lookout, Seaman William Lander, communicated to the Officer of the Deck (OOD), Ensign Dennis H. Biwerse, "Sir, I see a group of Jap airplanes approaching—about five thousand feet. They are in the 'vee' formation."

"How many airplanes, Lander?"

Lander looked through his binoculars. "Can't tell exactly. There are two groups. Perhaps ten or twelve."

"What type are they?"

"Can't tell."

"Keep me posted."

"Aye, aye, sir."

Seconds later, Lander reported, "I have them, sir. It's nine Nakajima, A4N, Type 95 navy biplanes* (131) and three Yokosuka, B4Y, Type-96 navy dive bombers."* (132)

"Very well." The OOD made notes in the ship's log. "Lookout, how many Jap formations have you spotted today?"

Landers responded, "Sir, this group is the fifth. But it's the first one with Jap navy aircraft."

"Understand." He completed his notations in the log and snapped it closed.

The Japanese bomb exploded dead center atop the wheelhouse. Fire, shrapnel, and wood splinters ripped into Commander Hughes, sending him into shock. Ensign Biwerse was hit in the back and both legs, crippling him. Shrapnel and glass shards slashed into Chief Quartermaster John H. Lang, our navigator. Lang, bleeding from numerous lacerations, tended to Hughes and Biwerse as best he could.

A second bomb smashed into the quarterdeck. A dozen more men were wounded, several seriously. The concussion slammed our executive officer, Lieutenant Arthur "Tex" Anders, against the aft bulkhead, knocking him unconscious and ripping his uniform to shreds.

Other bombs hit close aboard starboard. The *Panay* rocked back and forth and the vibrations on the deck from the engines ceased. Splinters cut down Lieutenant Junior Grade Clark Geist, our gunnery officer, as he was trying to get the tarpaulin off one of the 30-caliber machine guns.

Chief Boatswain's Mate Halhmann, though seriously wounded, clambered onto the remains of the bridge, assessed the damage, and realized that all the ship's officers were seriously wounded and out of action. He shouted over the din to the partially conscious commanding officer, Commander Hughes, "By your leave, Captain, I have command of the *Panay*."

He placed his boatswain's pipe* (133) close to his lower lip and blew the shrill tones for General Quarters over the 1MC communication system. He followed that in a stern and clear voice, "General Quarters. General Quarters. Man your battle stations. Man your battle stations." Again, he sent the boatswain's pipe's signal, and announced, "This is not a drill. Not a drill. General Quarters, General Quarters! All hands, man your battle stations. All hands, man your battle stations. Up and forward."

'Boats' Halhmann triggered the klaxon horn. Its loud, irritating, sharp groans blared throughout our ship. The crew, wounded and not, grabbed their World-War-One-era helmets,* (134) dogged the watertight hatches, and scrambled to their battle stations.

The civilians scurried for cover. The newsreel cameramen exposed several hundred feet of 35mm black-and-white film. Shrapnel wounded the two newsreel cameramen but they continued filming, and they captured key scenes of the Japanese attack.

Chief Halhmann spoke in a measured and positive voice over the 1MC, "All hands. Now hear this. All hands. Now hear this. The skipper and the all ship's officers are disabled. As the senior enlisted man in the ship's company, I have taken command of the *USS Panay*. I'm counting on all hands to do your duty."

Halhmann ordered the special sea and anchor detail deck crew to weigh anchor. He grabbed the handles on the engine-room telegraph, shoved them forward to the stop, and then back swiftly to "Slow Ahead."

Chief Machinist Mate Emery Fisher responded over the voice tube, "Aye, skipper, slow ahead. We got multiple damage in the engine room. Only one screw turning slowly. Take a bit to get more power. Will do soonest."

Our new skipper ordered the helmsman, "Hard to port." He knew how badly wounded the *Panay* was, and he wanted to beach ship on shore.

Seaman Cecil Speen, wounded in the upper chest and right arm, and with nicks in his forehead, wiped the blood from his eyes. "Aye, aye, sir." Straining, he eased the reluctant wheel slightly to port. "Chief, my error, skipper, the rudder is not responding. We're not moving and we're drifting with the current."

Chief Machinist Mate Peter Lumpers's damage-control crew worked below decks to control flooding and to repair damage.

Additional bombs exploded close aboard sending shards, splinters, and waves of water into the ship.

The gunner's mates' gang ripped the tarpaulins off the eight Lewis 30-caliber machine guns.* (135) Unfortunately, the machine guns were mounted for ground attack and the crew could not elevate them high enough to send effective anti-aircraft fire. Gunner's Mate Second Class John Hennessy and Gunner's Mate Third Class John Bonkoski wrestled two machine guns from their mounts, wrapped wet towels around their hands, and commenced firing. Unfortunately, to no avail, apparently. The Japanese naval aircraft pressed their attack.

A concussion blew the door off my radio shack and knocked me into the radio equipment, inflicting a bleeding gash on my forehead. Splinters hit me in my left arm and hand, my back and left leg. I used my right hand to press my handkerchief to the leg wound to stem the bleeding. I climbed onto my chair, took several deep breaths, and began tapping on the telegraph key, transmitting SOS messages over long-range radio waves on the maritime guard frequency. Soon, I began transmitting voice, "May Day, May Day, May Day" on 500 kilocycles, the international distress frequency. After a few seconds, I dialed the tuner to the Asiatic Fleet's guard frequency and began voice broadcasting a running account of this Japanese aerial attack.

Three or four of the Nakajima strafed the *Panay* with their twin 7.7mm machine guns. Bullets raked the *Panay* from bow to stern, hitting many of the ship's company.

Storekeeper First Class Charles Ensminger manned his battle station, the aft 30mm machine gun. With part of the tarpaulin hanging off the stand, he commenced firing at the low-level strafing Nakajima. Within seconds, bullets ripped into his chest. He slipped to the deck with his eyes open.

Bullets hit three machine-gunners and they fell to the deck. I had recovered enough to be ambulatory. I stumbled to an unmanned gun and starting firing. To what end, I do not know. Within a few minutes I lost consciousness and fell to the deck. Someone dumped water on me and slapped my cheeks. The world spun crazily as I recovered. I crawled into the radio shack.

Several more bombs exploded close aboard on our starboard, sending columns of water cascading onto our ship. Shards everywhere cut into the crew. The concussions separated plates on the hull below decks, causing flooding in the engine room. Chief Machinist Mate Vernon Pucket and his "snipe" gang stuffed mattresses into the holes in the hull to control the flooding.

Pucket shouted into the voice tube to the bridge, "Skipper, we're flooding. Doing the best we can to control it. Our pumps can't make headway." Suddenly, a part of the starboard hull gave way. The waters of the Yangtze quickly flooded the engine room and all ship's power was lost. The "snipe" crew and Chief Pucket scrambled up the ladders and dogged the hatches.

Another bomb smashed into the main deck close to Sick Bay and seriously wounded Pharmacist's Mate First Class James Steel. Nonetheless, he continued to tend to the wounded as best he could with his limited resources. He administered morphine to his shipmates who were in agonizing pain.

Shrapnel and splinters from another bomb slashed into the radio room, smashed into my left shoulder and side, and threw me against the aft bulkhead. I was bleeding profusely, and in mild shock. My assistant, Radioman Third Class James Murphy, his uniform covered in blood from multiple wounds, staggered into the radio room. As best he could, he wrapped a towel around my arm to stem the bleeding and forced me to drink water. The *Panay* was listing to starboard. Murphy helped me to my station and, without authorization and with no power, I connected the battery-powered backup radio and began tapping on the telegraph key to send the Morse code "SOS" distress signal over the guard channel. What the Hell! This was no time for formal naval procedures. In the Navy, initiative counts. Within a couple of minutes, I collapsed due to the loss of blood and intense pain.

It was 1540 hours. We were unable to get underway; the *Panay's* bow was awash and had a twelve-degree starboard list. Skipper Halhmann instructed Signalman First Class Harry Tuck and Seaman Charles Schroyer to pass the word to abandon ship. Tuck rang the ship's bell continuously, as hard as he could, and shouted into the dead 1MC, "Abandon ship. All hands, abandon ship." Schroyer dashed through the sinking ship shouting, "Abandon ship. All hands abandon ship."

The deck crew floated the ship's two motor launches—both damaged—and loaded the seriously wounded and the civilians aboard. Coxswains Walter Cheathman and Edgar Hulsebus helmed the launches back and forth to the river bank evacuating the crew and civilians. Two of the gunner's mates carried their Thompsons.

The Type 96 fighter planes strafed the motor launches en route to shore. On the second trip, bullets hit Hulsebus in the right side of his chest and right leg. Mustering all his mental and physical strength, he continued the ferrying operations until, on the next trip, he collapsed unconscious. Fireman First Class Davis Newton grabbled the tiller, took command of the launch, and helmed it to shore. Hulsebus died onshore. Newton continued command of the launch until the last person was ashore.

Once near the bank, the survivors hid in the deep mud and weeds along the bank, and tended the seriously wounded. Japanese naval infantry and soldiers on the shore sniped at the survivors. Several sailors took hits. Pharmacist Mate First Class James Steel, bleeding from numerous wounds, dispensed what tender loving care he had remaining.

Chief Halhmann saw that most of the ship's company and civilians were ashore. He ordered Coxswain Morris Rider to evacuate the wounded officers. Rider and several of the remaining crew loaded Lieutenant Commander Hughes on a stretcher. He protested, "I will be the last to leave the *Panay.*"

Chief Halhmann responded, "With respect, sir, now I am the commanding officer of the *USS Panay,* and I will see that all hands are away."

Hughes nodded his head slightly and closed his eyes, and the sailors carried Hughes and the other wounded officers to the last remaining motor launch, such as it was. Chief Halhmann struggled to walk along the steeply tilted main deck to ensure that all hands had abandoned ship. Satisfied, he climbed aboard the launch and Seaman Rider helmed it to shore. About halfway, Chief Halhmann stood and saluted the sinking *USS Panay.*

A Japanese patrol boat approached the *Panay.* An officer onboard saw that the ship was abandoned and sinking, and sailed away—offering no assistance, as is the law of the sea.

The last I recall was that I was in the river and someone was pulling me ashore. I watched as the *USS Panay* rolled over to starboard and slipped beneath the dark waters of the Yangtze.

The Japanese aircraft continued their attack on the Standard Oil Socony Vacuum Company's tankers—sinking the *Mei an,* mortally wounding Captain Peter Mender and many Chinese civilians, and inflicting serious casualties among the crew and passengers of all four tankers.

Army Captain Roberts, fluent in Mandarin, volunteered to go inland and find help. Eventually, he had a group of Chinese farmers assisting the survivors with blankets, food, and potable water.

Haunting us was the unknown: Had our SOSs reached an Occidental warship or a friendly radio receiver and, if so, was someone en route to rescue us?

Finally, two days later, 15 December, the American gunboat *USS Oahu** and the British gunboats *HMS Bee* and *Ladybird* arrived. All hands worked to transfer the *Panay's* crew to these ships. The Japanese Army promised safe passage, and the ships sailed for the International Settlement in Shanghai to transfer the wounded to hospitals.

FOURTEEN

American Embassy, Tokyo, December 1937

In Tokyo, Ambassador Joseph Grew* (136) lodged a formal protest about the attack on the *USS Panay* with the Japanese Foreign Minister Hirto Koki.* (137)

Minster Koki said that the attack on the *USS Panay* was a result of "mistaken identity."

We do not have an exact record of Ambassador Grew's response. But, I reckon that it was unsuitable for small children's ears.

The sinking of the *Panay* and the killing and wounding of our sailors caused an uproar back home, and initiated a serious diplomatic battle between the U.S.A. and the Empire of Japan. Fortunately, President Franklin Roosevelt* (137A) did not take the bait. He was well aware that the attack on the *Panay* was a gambit to entice America into a Pacific War. Japan's military was strong and aggressive, and ours was exceptionally weak.

Four months later, Vice Admiral Rokuzo Sugiyama* (138) extended a formal apology to Secretary of State Cordell Hull,* (138A) and offered a $2.2 million indemnity. President Roosevelt accepted the Japanese explanation, announced that the attack on the *USS Panay* was an unfortunate "incident" on the Yangtze, and the episode was closed.

After the end of the Pacific War, the Navy's Board of Inquiry released an unclassified report stating that Colonel Kingoro* (129) of the Imperial Japanese Army had ordered his artillery company to fire on the *Panay* convoy because he wanted to provoke the United States into a Pacific war he knew that the Empire of Japan would soon control the Pacific to the Hawaiian Islands and perhaps beyond.

And that's how it happened. As it were. By the by, I own a bridge in Brooklyn that's for sale—any of you readers interested? I'll make a sweet deal.

FIFTEEN

Retrospective view of the Japanese attack on the USS Panay

With the advantage of hindsight and the declassification of Top Secret intelligence, I may tell you what I reckon was the real reason for the Japanese attack on the *USS Panay*. The Japanese messages the morning of 12 December 1937 were in a simple tactical code that we had broken several months earlier. Before the first bomb hit my ship, several coded, tactical Japanese messages were on my desk. The codebreakers at Station Hypo, Pearl Harbor, uncorked these messages several days later.

Prince Yasuhiko Asaka, commander of the Japanese forces in the Nanking environs, had requested that Rear Admiral Mitsuami Teizo, the senior naval officer in the area, launch anti-ship air attacks on the Occidental convoy in the Yangtze. The Prince offered that, "All Army aircraft are engaged in supporting our ground troops (in the battle for Nanking)." Japanese intelligence said that the Standard Oil Socony Vacuum tankers carried aviation gasoline for the Chinese Air Force and that the ships in the convoy were transporting retreating Chinese soldiers.

Rear Admiral Teizo, concerned about this seriousness of this unprecedented hostile action against neutral ships, telephoned the Prince for confirmation. The Prince reaffirmed his order. Accordingly, Teizo tasked navy Captain Miki Morihiko* (139) with planning and executing the assault. In the navy's attack gaggle were three Yokosuka B4Y1, Type 96, biplane dive bombers—each carrying six 113-pound bombs; and nine Nakajima A4N, Type 95, biplane fighters, each with twin 7.7mm machine guns.

I've researched the classified intelligence, and I categorically affirm that Prince Yasuhiko fabricated his information. It was his *raison d'être* for ordering the attack on our Occidental convoy—an act of war. His hatred of the "white devils" is well documented.

I would suggest that you go to Chapter Twenty for additional details of Prince Yasuhiko's chicanery. Page XXX.

SIXTEEN

US Navy Hospital, Subic Bay, Commonwealth of the Philippines,
early February 1938

That shrapnel gash on my left leg was infected. The medicos worked diligently to prevent gangrene from developing. One morning in early February, the doctor, Commander Henry Walsh, and a cadre of nurses, corpsmen, and whatever, surrounded my bed. Doctor Walsh read my chart.

"What is this parade about?" I said to no one in particular, and got no response.

Walsh made a hand signal and a corpsman began cutting away the bandages around my leg. Most uncomfortable, I might add. The doc inspected the wound and uttered his usual medical jargon—gobbledygook to me.

"Chief Marne, that infection on your leg is stubborn and we're not making progress in curing it. We've identified the pathogen, but we've no specific curative to treat it. I'm stumped."

"What's the plan, Commander?"

"We'll keep trying, Marne. However, I must give you a 'heads up.' Should gangrene develop, we'll have to amputate. Otherwise, you'll meet Davy Jones the hard way."

How's that for good news this bright sunny morning? "Commander Walsh, that's not going to happen. By hook or crook, I'll cure that damn infection," I said with a touch of bravado. My heart sank. My career, and all my post-Navy plans would be dumped in the trash bucket. Veronica. Doctor Walsh and most of his gang left.

Without comment, the corpsman bandaged the leg. Leaving, he gave me the thumbs up sign, and said, "Dong hoa." That's Chinese. Could mean most anything. But I'll focus on 'Good luck' or 'Well done.'

I vowed not to get depressed. I smiled as images of Veronica danced in my mind. That was better. A few minutes later, the Filipino aide entered the ward with the library cart. At my bed, he said, "Mister Marne, what would you want today?"

"Anything new."

He handed me a couple of magazines, and ambled to the next bed. I tossed the magazines on my sideboard, and decided that a mid-morning nap with dreams of Veronica was appropriate. Very nice. Very nice, indeed. After lunch, I picked up one of the publications. It was a medical journal. Egad! I flipped the pages, looked at the pictures, and tossed it aside.

Chief Boatswain Mate Earnest Halhmann was in the next bunk. He was to be discharged in a few days, ready for duty. He overheard Commander Walsh's comments. He ambled to my bed and said, "Marne, I'll piss on that wound and then rub it down with used tobacco juice. That's what we used back home in Utah. Works on most anything—except maybe a diamondback strike."

That brought a chuckle. Then I realized he was serious. "Chief, surely you jest. If I had the faintest belief that your used tobacco juice would help this damn infection, I'd urge you to get a plug and start chewing."

Several minutes later, a *deus ex machina* was at my bedside and lit brightly that phantom light bulb over my head. A couple of months earlier, I had decoded a message, in a simple code, from the medical officer in the French colonial office in Saigon to the senior *Deuxième Bureau* officer in the French Embassy in Berlin. She had commented that the sample of that experimental Bayer AG drug was highly effective in combating infected wounds in the Legionnaires. "Would you task a *Bureau* agent to purloining another cache? How difficult is it to elude the Nazi Gestapo? The fighting with the Viet Minh has eased for now. If the ceasefire holds, I'll have enough of this drug to last for some time. If not, I'll need more soon."

Life was good. The *deus ex machina* had arrived on my stage. "Chief Halhmann, how about some assistance?"

"Sure, Marne. What's up?"

"I'm going to the intelligence spaces and I'll need your help."

"You're not fit to go anywhere. You nuts?"

"Chief, this plan I've conjured may be my last opportunity to save my leg."

"You spooks are nutty. What's the idea?"

"Help me with these crutches."

"You don't have a chit to leave this hospital. You'll be tagged with an unauthorized absence and get a Captain Mast. And so will I. You're out of uniform in those Navy issue PJs and bathrobe."

"Indeed, you are correct. Let's shove off."

No one challenged us as we walked out of the ward, down the aisle, into the rotunda, and out the front door. Chief Halhmann hailed a jitney.

We got some curious eyes en route and in the headquarters building. The OOD gave me a hard time. Chief Halhmann intervened and the fellow let us pass with a stern warning. Down the hall, down the ladder, down another very long passageway in the basement. At the green door, I asked Chief Halhmann if he would mosey about. "Don't know how long it will take." I pushed the buzzer.

The peephole opened and a familiar voice said, "Marne, what the Hell you doing here? You're out of uniform. Come in."

No need to tell you all the details. Here's the essence of my scheme. Everything was back-channel and unauthorized. As luck would have it, the naval attaché at our consulate in Saigon was Marine Major Arthur MacGregor—an ol' China hand. He and I had served in our consulate in Peiping. He knew the French female doctor—not intimately, I reckon.

The day after he received our message, Major MacGregor took the lady doctor to dinner, laced with a bottle or two of Mumm's finest. Afterwards, the doctor was pleased to show Major MacGregor her laboratory. MacGregor spotted three quart-size bottles containing a white powder labeled "Sulfonamide."* (140) The doctor was delighted to explain in detail how effectively this miracle drug killed infectious organisms.

Standing by was the Major's mercenary dacoit. Later that evening, one bottle of sulfonamide was on the major's desk, and the thief had a new U.S.A. $100 bill. Next morning, MacGregor, a naval aviator, piloted the attaché's newly arrived PBY Catalina* (140A) to Naval Air Station, Subic Bay.

End of story. The sulfonamide worked to a fare-thee-well. The infected wound healed quickly, and I was discharged. I was still using a cane, but I expected to junk it in a couple of months.

SEVENTEEN

US Navy Station, Subic Bay, Commonwealth of the Philippines,
February 1938

I had no uniform, no orders, no place to go, and nothing to do. Never in my career had I had so much free time. I was bored, hanging out in the Chief's quarters, sleeping, reading, swimming, and wondering what had happened to Veronica and her father. My sea bag, my haute wardrobe, and my personal gear were at the bottom of the Yangtze. My today wardrobe consisted of two sets of used dungarees, shoes, and a baseball cap.

One afternoon the messenger from the quarter deck found me in the recreation space. "Hey, Chief Marne, the disbursing clerk in headquarters wants to see you."

"Now?"

"Now. He's has your survivor's pay ready."

"I reckon that's now."

I'd never seen so much cash. Except for some spending money, all went into an account with a U.S.A. commercial bank. Just in case, I added my father's and mother's names to the account. Also got a chit for a full set of Chief Petty Officer's uniforms.

A few days later, a messenger from Communications brought me a Priority, Confidential message from the Director of Naval Intelligence, Rear Admiral Ralston Holmes, USN.* (141) I took the closest chair. Chief Petty Officers do not get messages from admirals. With a slightly shaky hand, I removed the message from the sealed envelope.

It was okay. He congratulated me for earning the Navy Cross, and was pleased that my wounds had completely healed. He'd been following my career, and he was impressed with my professionalism and ingenuity. "Off the record, Chief Marne, that *tour de force* you engineered to relieve that French doctor in Indochina of the sulfonamide was singularly inventive. Congratulations. And, I have your portfolio in our vault." Whoops!

"The Pacific war with the Empire of Japan is a sure thing and on the horizon. I need experienced career officers to bolster our growing service— especially those with China service. I will sponsor your commission as a Special Duty Officer, Intelligence Specialist, with the rank of Lieutenant, senior grade.* (142) I urge you to accept."

When Admirals urge, one accepts.

✳ ✳ ✳ ✳ ✳

I spent twelve weeks in "charm" school at the Naval Air Station, Pensacola.* (143) It was similar to boot camp, only sophisticated, as it were. Learned a lot: how to salute with my sword, the gentle manners of polite society, which fork goes where, how to address the Ambassador of Outer Baluchistan, what uniform to wear on what social occasion, small-arms training, naval-infantry tactics, a lot of physical training (my body was not ready for its intensity so I did low-strength exercises), lots of academic studies, Navy regulations, naval history, rhetoric, public speaking, and lots of other stuff. On the whole, it was sort of interesting. Actually, I was making the transition to commissioned officer with ease.

Graduation day was set for the first Saturday in May 1938. Mom rode the Sunset Limited from Alpine to New Orleans. She took the interstate bus to Pensacola. I met her at the station for a joyful reunion with lots of hugs and kisses. Dad was having arthritis problems, so he remained in Marfa and sent his love and best wishes. Graduation day was the first time I wore my dress whites with two gold stripes on my shoulder boards.* (144) I was on top of the world.

The Naval intelligence detailer sent message orders—report to the Navy School of Photography to attend the "B" class starting Monday, 6

June.* (145) No reason given. Fortunately, this school was at the air station at Pensacola. The only camera I had operated was a Kodak Brownie. Push the button and you've got a photograph. *Voila!* Six months later, I was a bona fide Navy photographer with a certificate to prove it.

EIGHTEEN

American Embassy, Tokyo, January 1939

My first assignment as a commissioned officer was to the naval attaché office in our embassy in Tokyo.* (146) My diplomatic credentials listed me as the deputy naval attaché. Actually, I was Ambassador Grew's troubleshooter. I traveled this island nation top to bottom, taking pictures with my new Leica 35mm camera* (147) of the scenery (I reckon that you understand "scenery"). No matter where I went, I was accompanied 'tailed' by a couple of Black Dragon thug* (148) and occasionally they would manhandle me—notwithstanding my diplomatic immunity.

For instance, late one evening in June 1939, I was in Kyoto photographing the Kiyonizu Dera Temple, an innocent pastime.* (149) The thugs knocked me to the ground and stole my Leica. No serious harm done and no need for an official protest—that's the way the Japanese intelligence service operates.

Pacific War clouds became increasingly more ominous. One of our primary goals in a diplomatic mission is to look after American citizens in the host country. Oftentimes, I'd visit Japanese American citizens working or visiting relatives in Japan. I'd warn them about Japanese aggression and the deteriorating relations between our countries, and encourage them to return to the United States. I took their photographs, and made fingerprints. My concluding remarks were, "If you are in the Empire of Japan after the war starts, you will be interned. The Kenpeitai (Japanese secret police* (150) will accuse you of being a spy and will interrogate you with acutely painful methods. You will confess to whatever they want you to say. Those that they truly suspect of being American agents will undergo a more horrific interrogation and then be beheaded. Eligible males will be forced into the Imperial Japanese Army." Unfortunately, few of these Japanese Americans heeded my warning.

It was the Fourth of July, 1939, and Ambassador Grew was hosting a formal ball and dinner to celebrate the birthday of the United States of America. The guests included senior Japanese government officials, military officers, industrialists, and principal officials from other embassies. It was a gala affair, indeed. The Marine band, dressed in their formal scarlet uniforms,* (151) played a repertoire of waltzes, big-band tunes, Latin rhythms, and most anything else. At the reception, the butler served the finest champagnes from New York and California. However, unbeknownst to Ambassador Grew, the butler, an ingenious fellow, had secreted several dozen cases of premium French Mumm Grand Cordon Stellar. He ordered the Mumm wine served with the dinner. The compliments overwhelmed the ambassador.

I wore my summer mess-dress uniform,* (152) and was seated at Ambassador Grew's table. Across the table and a few chairs away, I spotted Prince Yasuhiko Asaka. (I withheld my rage and killer urge.) I nodded to the Prince in acknowledgement. He did not return my courtesy. Instead, he turned to the woman seated to his left and spoke to her *sotto voce*. The woman was an Oriental beauty (as only an Oriental woman can be) and she was dressed in an enticing evening gown—custom designed in Paris, no doubt. That gown emphasized her every curve. In fact, it revealed far more of her curves than it ought.

I ignored the pair, and chatted with my dinner companion, a *femme d'une certaine âge* who worked in our communication section. And I made fitting comments to our guests seated in my vicinity. The music was infectious, wine delightful, and all in all, the good times suffused throughout the embassy. But something in the back of my mind kept vexing me. For a reason I cannot explain, I looked again at the Prince's female companion. She returned the glance, looked briefly at her plate, and beckoned a server to fill the prince's glass. A short time later, a mental image arose. That woman had been my classmate in the Japanese language course. No comments, if you please.

NINETEEN

American Embassy, Tokyo, June 1939

One morning in late June 1939, Ambassador Grew sent an aide to fetch me from the communication room, my workplace. In his office, he handed me a message from Rear Admiral Walter S. Anderson, DNI (Director of Naval Intelligence).* (153) The admiral notified me that, effective immediately, I had been promoted to the rank of lieutenant commander.* (154) Ambassador Grew shook my hand and said, "Well deserved, Lieutenant Commander Marne. Congratulations."

Whoops! Something was afoot, as detective Holmes was wont to say. I'd been commissioned for only eighteen months, and promotions in the peacetime Navy took years in grade. I learned many years ago that there is a balance in all human endeavors—especially in the United States Navy. A *quid pro quo*, as it were.

The ambassador continued, "Admiral Anderson has tasked me to send you on a special assignment, and it requires an officer with senior rank."

Here comes the other shoe drop. "Ambassador, please continue."

He cleared his throat. "Everything said next is classified Top Secret, code Uranus."

Okay, folks, here it comes. "Yes, sir. I understand."

"You are going to Manchukuo as a guest of the Empire of Japan. Actually, your destination is the border between the People's Republic of Mongolia and Manchukuo. You are an accredited observer of the undeclared war between the Imperial Japanese Eighth Army* (155) and the military forces of the Union of Socialist Soviet Republics* (156) over a border dispute near the Nomonhon village in Manchukuo."* (157) He paused to gather his thoughts. "In that godforsaken part of our planet, who gives a damn? Anyway, those fellows have been scuffling over that border, the Chinese Eastern Railway,* (158) Korea, and just about everything else ever since the defeat of the Russian navy at the battle of Tsushima Strait in 1905."* (159) He looked at me with those penetrating eyes of his. "Questions, Marne?"

"Not yet, Ambassador." Actually, I was numb. I was going to Mongolia as a guest of the Japanese. Whoops! Something was going askew, and I reckoned it would be me.

The ambassador continued. "It took some serious doing but we persuaded Field Marshal Hajime Sugiyama, Chief of Staff of the Japanese imperial army,* (160) to sanction your observer status. You will be my personal representative with full diplomatic immunity."

That was it, folks. What the Hell did naval intelligence need to know about a nonsense, undeclared war in a place no civilized society gave a hoot about? Those Japanese bastards knew my background and would capture me to get the Navy's secrets. Damn. I was getting flustered and nonsensical over what could be a dynamite assignment, as it were.

"My chauffeur, in the official embassy automobile, will drive you to the Japanese Navy airfield at Atsugi, about sixteen miles south of Yokohama. Sometime during the day you will board a Mitsubishi GM4, twin-engine aircraft,* (161) and be en route to Changchun, Manchukuo's capitol city."

"What specifically am I to observe? And what am I to do about it, sir?"

Sensing my feeble attempt at polite cheekiness, he continued with that crooked smile of his, "Use your new Leica* (162) with all those lenses and take numerous photographs and copious notes, and keep the exposed film and notes in your locked diplomatic pouch. We'll process the film in the Navy's laboratory in the basement."

"I understand."

"Naval intelligence wants to know about the Japanese command and control structure, intelligence proficiency and field capabilities, speed and execution of orders by subordinate units, initiative and decision making by field commanders, discipline, training and fighting spirit of the troops, weapons and how they function, treatment of prisoners of war, and anything interesting."

"Mister Ambassador, I have a few questions."

"Very well, Lieutenant Commander Marne."

"How long is this assignment?"

"Until their war is over or when we recall you."

"Do I speak Japanese or English?

"Japanese at all times."

"Do I go in mufti or wear my Navy uniform?"

"You represent the United States of America. Uniform at all times. I suggest you wear dress khakis. The weather is mild and at night that is a chill in that desert."

"How do we communicate and on what schedule?"

"Excellent point, Marne. Most likely, we don't. Perhaps, however, from time to time you can persuade a Japanese radio operator to send a message to me via American Express in Tokyo using the Radio Corporation of America's link. In any case, keep such messages short. Tell us where you are, about your well-being, and how many rolls of film you've exposed. Nothing else."

"Should I take my 1911 Colt 45?"

"Absolutely not. You are not a combatant. If it becomes necessary to defend yourself, I suppose the Japanese will lend you a weapon of some sort."

"Yes, sir," I said, with a hint of incredulity. Ain't that sweet? I've got an irate Russki charging with a fixed bayonet, determined to impale me to kingdom come, and I've gotta ask some Japanese trooper passing by, "Sir, please lend me your rifle, I'll return it, after I dispatch this fellow with the black beard." Folks, have I ever told you about that bridge I have for sale?

I might have been dumb, but I wasn't stupid. For the first time in my career, I disobeyed a direct order. I stowed my 1911 Colt 45, three extra clips, and a box of ammo in my duffle—a part of my diplomatic pouch. I was not going into a war zone naked, as it were.

The road trip to Atsugi was uneventful. At the airfield, the base commander, an Imperial Japanese Navy captain, was waiting for us. A junior officer opened the automobile door, saluted, and escorted me to meet the captain. I saluted. The captain returned my salute, bowed several times, and said, "Welcome, Lieutenant Commander Matthew Marne of the United States Navy, honored guest of the Empire of Japan, to Naval Air Base Atsugi." He smiled slightly. "We are pleased that you will see how the aggressive Soviet army encroaches into Manchukuo, takes our water from the Khalkyn Gol, steals our cattle, and harasses our citizens." He bowed a couple times and continued from the script. "Our army fights bravely and defeats the invaders in every battle."

Clearly the fellow was reciting the propaganda written for my arrival. I acknowledged his greeting with the best smile I could muster. "Captain, it is my pleasure to be a guest of the Empire of Japan, and I shall observe assiduously the heroic Japanese army repulsing the Communist forces of the Union of Soviet Socialist Republics."

He invited me to enter his automobile and we drove to Base Operations Terminal. Got lots of curious looks—some hostile. On arrival, the captain introduced me to my escort. "I have chosen Lieutenant James Akira to be your escort. He is a Christian, intelligent, brown belt First Kyu,* (163) and he is eager to assist you."

Lieutenant Akira stepped forward, saluted, bowed several times and spoke in excellent English. "Good afternoon, Mister Marne. I am pleased to be your escort while you are the guest of Japan. Please ask, and I shall accomplish."

I returned his salute. I should not have been surprised. These Japanese naval officers were top notch. And the use of "Mister" was in-sightful. (Following the British tradition, U.S. Naval officers below the rank of commander are addressed as "Mister.") Akira was probably a naval intelligence officer. So what, so am I. In my imperfect Japanese I replied, "Lieutenant Akira, it is my pleasure to meet you. We'll get along famously swapping sea stories. And, please, let us dispense with all this saluting. Agree?"

Akira guided me through the waiting room that was jammed with soldiers in full kit—en route to Mongolia, no doubt. He indicated that the VIP room was at the top of the stairs. "I shall conduct you to the GM4 aircraft in about two hours in the future."

The VIP room was large, decorated in formal Japanese style, and had several side rooms furnished with tatami mats. A sliding door could isolate each room. I was greeted by a charming female dressed in formal kimono. She bowed four or five times and said, "*Konnichiwa.*" (Good afternoon). The rest of her message was mostly garbled English. I reckon she meant "Lieutenant Commander Marne, United States Navy." However, her "How may I serve you?" was well said and the double entendre was all too obvious. I responded in Japanese, "Tea and rice cakes, *dŏ ka.*" (Please).

Shortly, she returned and served the refreshments. Afterwards, she moved to the far corner of the room and began playing music on the three-stringed shamisen.* (164)

At 1545 exactly, Akira entered and guided me to a Japanese Mitsubishi G4M1 aircraft parked on the ramp about fifty yards or thereabouts from Operations. The ramp was crowded with all manner of Japanese war planes. Their empennage, painted in diagonal orange stripes, indicated that we were Mongolia bound.* (165) Akira carried my duffel bag, and I toted the small diplomatic pouch. I entered through the small door on the port side and was amazed. This was an executive aircraft fit for the elite traveler. The interior, fitted out as a Japanese tea house, had only two comfortable seats.

Akira moved into the cockpit. That was a puzzlement. James Akira a naval aviator? He was not wearing wings on his uniform. Flight engineer? Or, he was not allowed in the VIP section so he was ensconced in a jump seat. Reckon, that's it.

The comely stewardess was dressed in a chic Western-style uniform. She offered all manner of snacks (Japanese style) and beverages. I declined, and stayed with the tried and true tea and rice cakes.

The takeoff was smooth and the climb to cruise altitude was "gentle." The five-hour trip was uneventful. No need to detail the rest of my journey to the war zone. Nothing of significance to report—routine via Japanese

Army transportation: railroad, aircraft, automobile, and truck. Throughout the journey, I was keenly aware that the Kenpeitai documented my every move.* (166)

TWENTY

Nomonhan, Manchukuo. June 1939

Nomonhan village was a collection of Mongolian yurts,* (167) a few dusty streets, several wood structures, and a mud brick dispensary. The Khalkhyn Gol was a wide, shallow, muddy river. And that was about it. Nothing else around for miles, except the consummately-awful desert of no import. Couldn't see what the fuss was about. I wouldn't have given four bits for it, as far my eyes could see.

Nonetheless, the Japanese and Soviet combatants fought furiously: for pride and revenge, for the most part, most likely. Airplanes, tanks, and artillery did what they do best, and the foot soldiers suffered the incoming. The battle raged back and forth across the Khalkhyn Gol for several months. The carnage was staggering and bodies lay where they fell—stinking mess. I had to admire the Japanese infantryman. He was brave to a fault. He fought to his death with all his will and might; to die for the Emperor would bring him and his family honor.

Folks, there was no way I was going to put my body into that killing maw. My guide and I established my 'digs' in a tent on a small knob behind the village. With my binoculars, I could see what needed to be seen. When the fighting had abated, I would wander through the Japanese trenches, and chat with troopers and their officers. I snapped their pictures, and pictures of the carnage, damaged equipment, and Soviet prisoners. I exposed a dozen rolls of film through my Leica. Some of those shots ought to satisfy the intel poohbahs at Pearl.

By late July, the Japanese army had established a strong bridgehead across the Khalkhyn Gol into the People's Republic of Mongolia, and was ready to give the Red Army the *coup de grâce*.

Alarmed, Josef Stalin,* (168) General Secretary of the Communist Party's Central Committee of the Union of Soviet Socialist Republics (how about 'Dictator of the Soviet Union'), ordered Marshal Gregori Zhukov* (169) to gather a strong military force from the European sector and defeat the Japanese. (If not, it would be the Lubyanka Prison* (170) for Zhukov and a bullet to the head—as most of the Red Army senior officers experienced in Stalin's purges in the '30s..) Soon, the Trans-Siberian railroad was surfeited with trains transporting troops, weapons, supplies, and whatever to Zhukov's Red army in Mongolia.

In the dark, early morning hours of 20 August 1939, Marshal Zhukov launched his counter offensive. Massed Soviet artillery* (171) opened with a murderous barrage of unprecedented intensity. Two hours later, the massed Soviet infantry advanced: through the bridgehead, across the river, over Japanese trenches, into Nomonhan and beyond. Zhukov's Red army had overrun the remnants of the Japanese Twenty-Third Division—resulting in its total destruction.

Several days earlier, in anticipation of the expected Soviet offensive, I'd planted a medium-size American flag on a staff in front of my tent. Nonetheless, several errant Soviet shells exploded in my area and I hit the deck. Shrapnel ripped through my tent. One shard hit Lieutenant Akira in his back. I wrapped a towel over the bloody wound and around his body. I hailed a medic, and his team carried Akira to an aid station. Folks, this was getting serious. I was a neutral and was in my dress khaki uniform of the United States Navy. I reached for my binoculars, Leica, and the 1911 Colt 45. It would be inopportune to document in this memoir what I saw and heard—not for the civilized.

A couple days later the battle was abating. Japanese troops, the few remaining, were trying to make a stand behind the village. Soviet troops were everywhere, and for the most part ignored me. Seeing that I was taking pictures with a professional camera, and that my pistol was holstered, they reckoned I was a war correspondent and let me be.

Unfortunately, one dumb-ass Soviet trooper reckoned incorrectly. When I spotted him, he was about ten yards away and running directly at me. He stopped, raised his rifle to his right shoulder and pointed it towards me. Suddenly, I was a combatant, and my 1911 Colt 45 spoke three times. Crisis over.

I saved my life but the ruckus and the dead Soviet at my feet attracted attention that I could have done without. A senior officer (major perhaps) approached, pointed his pistol at my chest, and pointed to my 1911 Colt 45. I gave it to him handle first—just like the white-hatted cowboys did in the Hopalong Cassidy motion pictures.* (171A) He asked a barrage of questions in Russian—a language in which I have no skills, save *nostrovia*. To make a long story short, the fellow arrested me. His aide searched me, found my ID card, immunity documents, and my orders signed by Ambassador Grew. On the major's orders, a couple of his privates ransacked what was left of my tent and returned with what was left of my kit in the duffle, my flat hat, diplomatic pouch, and the American flag.

The Nomonhan war was over, but I was in deep trouble—an American naval officer probably facing Soviet justice on a murder charge. Folks, I got to tell you, the comedian W. C. Field's* (172) famous quote, "On the whole, I'd rather be in Philadelphia," was dead-on.

I was loaded onto a truck, driven to Soviet headquarters—now on the Manchukuo side of the river, and led inside a large tent with the hammer-and-sickle flag prominent. Several senior Red officers were about. Lying on a small stand were my ID card, papers, 1911 Colt 45, binoculars, Leica, film pouch, flag, and my uniform khaki flat hat. The diplomatic pouch and duffle, such as they were, were on the floor leaning against the stand. In a few minutes, Marshal Grigori Zhukov entered and said in passible English, "So you are the American who murdered my soldier."

I stood at attention and saluted him.

He roared, "This is a war zone. No formalities here." He lit a cigarette; its smoke smelled like fresh cow dung. "First, who are you and what are doing here? Your absolute truth is essential."

"Marshal, if I may?" I nodded toward the stand.

Zhukov grunted, "да." (Yes.)

I handed him my Navy identification card and my orders signed by Ambassador Grew: "I am Lieutenant Commander Matthew Marne of the United States Navy and I'm in Manchukuo as a neutral observer with diplomatic immunity."

"Yes, yes, yes," Zhukov growled. He picked up my 1911 Colt 45 in his left hand and sniffed the inside of the barrel. He smelt the gunpowder residue. "Why did you kill my soldier? Your Colt 45 was fired recently." He dropped the magazine and counted the bullets. "Three rounds gone." His black eyes narrowed, "Three 45-caliber bullets to kill one Russian. Must have been an Uzbek from the Caucasus—tough and mean."

I began to tell him I killed the Russian soldier in self-defense, but he cut me off at my first syllable.

"Who cares? What's another dead Russian? There are thousands of Russian corpses rotting out there in the desert. One more makes no difference. We have millions of them—good riddance of these peasants." He drew deeply on his cigarette and, as he let the smoke dribble out of his nose and the corners of his mouth, he stared appraisingly at me. "I like you, American naval intelligence officer. You have grit. You should be a senior officer in our Red Army." He paused. Looked about to assess the scene. "But no matter." He nodded his head toward the stand. "Get your equipment."

I stowed the binoculars, my 1911 Colt 45, and my film bag in my duffle. I operated the Leica's shutter several times, and the film-advance mechanism. Worked okay.

The Marshal watched me carefully. "Spy camera?"

"No, sir. I used it to document facets of this war."

"So you are also a photographic journalist?" The eternal cigarette flared as he took a deep drag. "A photographer! Want to take a photograph of me? Take it." A command.

I did the deed. He followed with, "Take photographs of the Red Army—soldiers alive and dead, our equipment, our tanks, our airplanes, anything."

My *deus ex machina* had arrived again, dressed in the uniform of a Soviet Field Marshal. Over the next couple of hours, I exposed four rolls of 36-exposure film. A *coup* I could not have envisioned. I did the photography to a fare-thee-well. My escort was a four-star general. No hindrances and full cooperation all 'round.

On my return, Marshal Zhukov left his staff meeting. "Satisfied, Lieutenant Commander Marne?"

"Yes, sir. Thanks for your suggestion and cooperation."

He jabbed his left index finger at my heart. "Send me prints. Yes."

"Sir, I will do just that. My word."

"I will send them to our NKVD, The People's Commissariat for Internal Affairs—Soviet intelligence.* (173) None of those fellows around here in the war zone." One of the staff officers approached and they conversed *soto voce* for a few seconds. Reckon they were being cautious about the possibility that I understood Russian. The Field Marshal issued an order, and the fellow decamped the tent post haste.

"Now, Lieutenant Commander Marne, we will drink to our great Soviet victory over those slant-eyed bastards in this damn desert. Now, we own the Khalkhyn Gol, Nomonhan, and thousands of hectares of Manchukuo or Manchuria, or whatever is correct. It is the first payback for our 1905 fiasco with these Orientals." He ordered his batman (or whatever it was in Russian) to fetch vodka, caviar, and rye toast with *crème fraiche.* "And there will be hundreds more paybacks, mark my words, American."

Folks, I fell into the rabbit hole at the Red Army Headquarters in Manchukuo. For the next several hours, it was bacchanal. I've never seen so many people drink so much vodka and still be standing. To be courteous and engender cordial relations, I must admit, I imbibed a tad—just a smidgeon, mind you. The balalaikas' strings spun forth enthralling music. And male and female soldiers danced frenetically. A Russian *soirée*, as it were.

The sun had set many hours earlier and the festivities continued apace. Frankly, I was slightly tipsy, tired, and longing for a spot to sleep. Marshal Zhukov grabbed my right arm. In a slightly slurred voice, he said, "Enjoying the Russian bash, American Marne?"

"Yes, sir. I'm fascinated with the festivities."

Zhukov grabbed a female dancer, kissed her on the lips, and patted her derriere. "That lovely woman is my assistant communication officer—the most talented in the Red Army."

I wondered. Was Zhukov boasting or sending me a message? "Marshal, if I am not under arrest, I should leave?"

"No! You are going to Moscow with me. I want to present you to Comrade Secretary Josef Stalin. To show him the mettle of the American naval officers—not the popinjays he believes the American military people are."

"Marshal Zhukov, I appreciate your invitation. But I must decline. I am scheduled to return to my duty station in Tokyo."

The cigarette danced in his left hand. In his no-nonsense voice he bellowed, "No invitation. You are under my protection and I take you to Moscow." He calmed. "You and I will become friends on the seven-day journey on the Trans-Siberian Railroad."

Next morning we were in Marshal Zhukov's Packard V12 limousine* (174) headed for the station at Erilian—a five-hour drive over Mongolian roads. Between the times he was on the radio to Moscow and various military facilities, he and I chatted about things of no import. We were well supplied with chilled vodka, caviar, rye bread and cheese. Accordingly, I might say, the journey was pleasant. The Marshal was supremely intelligent, innovative, empathetic, and a natural leader. I liked him. And hated his cigarettes.

At Erilian, his private train was ready. The locomotive's excess steam was hissing onto the station. The conductor was standing at attention, as were all other station and train personnel. Zhukov grabbed my arm. "Bring your camera and photograph my private car."

Folks, my vocabulary is inadequate to effectively describe the luxury of this railroad car's opulence. I reckon in the Soviet Union some comrades are more equal than other comrades. I took a dozen photographs of Zhukov's car, and I snapped several close-ups of him with my telephoto lens.

My duffle and the diplomatic pouch were on the station platform.

"With your permission, Marshal Zhukov, I'll get my kit. What car am I assigned?"

"My friend Matthew Marne, United States naval intelligence officer, I have changed my mind. Frankly, it was an inane idea to consider taking you to Moscow. The Third Reich has invaded Poland,* (175) and Great Britain and France have declared war on Germany. World War Two is underway. Soon, Hitler* (176) will order his Wehrmacht to invade the Soviet Union." He paused as if he were considering options, and lit another of those foul cigarettes. "No matter that you are my guest, Lavrentiy Beria* (177) would order the NKVD to arrest you, American intelligence officer. The secret police would torture you for your country's secrets, kill you with a bullet to back of the head in Lubyanka Prison, and destroy your remains in muriatic acid. The Soviet Union will aver that they never heard of you. And I will affirm that we released you and when last seen, you were hiking toward Nomonhan."

Clearly, Philadelphia was a more opportune destination. Marshal Zhukov was correct. I would disappear into the maw of the Red terror.

Zhukov continued, "I leave you here in Erilian, and I leave Senior Lieutenant Elizaveta Grekov here as your escort. She is fluent in English, Japanese, and some others I fail to recall. She will escort you to Vladivostok, where she will arrange your transport to Tokyo."

His routing confused my simple mind. "Marshal, may I suggest, from here the simplest route to Japan is via Peiping—only 500 miles distant. Why route me the long way around to Vladivostok?"

"Lieutenant Commander Marne of the United States Navy, the Japanese Kwangtung Army has occupied Peiping. You would not be welcomed, and the Kenpeitai probably would arrest and behead you."

Whoops! What was he saying? Nonsense. "Sir, I am an invited guest of the Empire of Japan traveling with diplomatic immunity. The Japanese will honor the international protocols."

The Marshal smashed his cigarette in an ashtray, and looked askance at me. "What a naive fellow you are, Marne. As, I suspect, are most Americans. The Japanese are devious bastards and cannot be trusted. And soon, I suspect, you will experience their chicanery. Mark my words."

I started to respond, but on a second's reflection kept my mouth closed.

Zhukov lit another cigarette and the fetid smoke fouled this luxurious car. "Listen carefully, my friend. The Japanese lost this small war here in Mongolia to their longtime nemesis, the Union of Soviet Socialist Republics, and they are shocked, bitter, and fuming in anger. Yesterday, my signals-intelligence officer reported that the Kenpeitai knows that you have my protection and that you've photographed my soldiers and military equipment, and they believe that you are a Soviet agent. His black eye narrowed. "To answer your unasked question, the Black Dragon Society has spies everywhere—even on my staff, perhaps, for a while longer."

Gadzooks! The Marshal was bubbling with challenging news, as it were. Where's the train to Philadelphia?

"To business. You will find Senior Lieutenant Grekov most capable in all things. Follow her lead precisely. No questions and no hesitation. Buy clothing in the town and wear it at all times in my country. Grekov also will travel in civilian clothes. Speak to no one. The NKVD is everywhere, and their zeal to discover anti-Soviet thought is dauntless, and would engender a Soviet justice you would do well to avoid."

"I understand, and will comply."

"Excellent."

He exhaled more cow-dung smoke, and I was going to be ill.

"I have instructed Grekov to buy a parlor ticket for the north-bound train to Irkutsk." He smiled faintly. "In this democratic socialist country, only the proletariat are privileged to purchase a steerage railroad ticket. You will change trains there. She will purchase a bedroom compartment for the very next train en route to Vladivostok. On the long journey to the Pacific, you will find Elizaveta Grekov a delightful traveling companion. You must tell me about it one day."

No response required and none offered.

He beckoned the officer sitting at a small desk in a far corner. In his no-nonsense voice the Marshal directed, "Captain Bykov, give Lieutenant Commander Marne 20,000 rubles,* (178) and 1,000 United States dollars in gold certificates.* (179) And 100,000 rubles to Senior Lieutenant Elizaveta Grekov. No receipts." He cracked a small embarrassed smile, "Our currency is not worth much."

He continued his instructions. "And complete an internal passport and travel permit for Lieutenant Commander Marne.* (180) Prepare travel orders, marked Secret, for Senior Lieutenant Elizaveta Grekov. And prepare, on my official Marshal of the Union of Soviet Socialist Republics stationery, a safe-passage transit document for these two. I will sign it."

He shook my hand vigorously. "I wish you good fortune, my American intelligence agent." Damn, he lit another of those cigarettes. In an empathetic voice that I had been unaware of until then, he said, "If we survive this coming war, we shall meet in Paris and toast to better times."

Note. I never saw Marshal Grigori Zhukov again. I did send him several hundred black-and-white prints of the Nomonhan adventure. I've wondered if he got them. *¿Quién sabe?*

TWENTY-ONE

American Embassy, Tokyo, November 1939

For six solid days, the Naval Attaché, Captain William Morrison, conducted my debriefing—recording my comments on wax cylinders in his Dictaphone. My camera logs were essential in facilitating my recall of the facts and evoking background information from my Nomonhon adventure. Meantime, in the Navy photographic laboratory, the mates processed forty-two rolls of black-and-white film and made contact sheets for us to peruse and decide what frames to print.

For the next couple of weeks, I was consumed with Nomonhan photography: reviewing the contact pints, ordering 8x10 enlargements, and writing the captions.

The attaché classified my bound Nomonhan report Secret. It was over one-hundred-thousand words long and included almost five hundred prints. Admiral James Richardson,* (181) Commander Battle Force, United States Fleet, sent a Consolidated PBY Catalina amphibian to Tokyo to transport my report, in a diplomatic pouch, to Pearl for intelligence review and forwarding to Naval Intelligence Headquarters in Washington.

Several days later, Ambassador Grew told me, "Admiral Richardson sent me a message this morning. He and his intelligence staff at Pearl Harbor are most pleased with your comprehensive report and on-target photographs of that Nomonhon war. He sends you his personal 'well done.'" Grew rose from his chair, grabbed my right hand, and shook it to a fare-thee-well. "Lieutenant Commander Marne, 'you done good,' as you Texans are apt to mouth. Get out of town for a few days and recuperate."

"Aye, aye, sir." That afternoon I was on the train to Kyoto, a beautiful city and the ancient home of the Chrysanthemum Throne of Japan. Naturally, my followers followed me. *C'est la vie.*

I booked a suite at the Kurama Omen Inn, noted for its hospitality and natural hot-spring baths. I'd requested a suite with a private hot-spring bath. I left my shoes at the door of my suite, donned a pair of tatami slippers, shed my clothes (save undershorts), donned a scarlet and dark blue kimono, collapsed into the soft bed, and slept the sleep of the mentally and physically exhausted.

A soft chime and a sweet, carefully modulated female voice awakened me. "Good morning, Matthew Marne. I have hot tea, sembei, and fresh fruit for you." Slowly, my reverie subsided and I returned to reality. This lovely female apparition was tending the blinds, and the soft morning sun brightened my suite. She was wearing a pastel blue kimono trimmed in bright pink. Egad! She was beautiful. Perhaps twenty years old, with dark-brown hair cut Western style and bright brown eyes, she moved with subtle grace.

"Good morning to you, *wakai josei.*" (young woman)

She knelt by the side of the bed. "My name is Michiko, and I'm your personal attendant." With a soft smile, she continued, "I am here to please you. You ask and I shall achieve."

"Please arise to enjoy hot-spring bath this fine morning." She slipped out of her kimono and *au naturel* eased her nearly-perfectly-formed body into the steaming waters. She smiled with those stunning brown eyes. "Please to join me."

I did.

✳ ✳ ✳ ✳ ✳

For the next several months, I traveled the Land of the Rising Sun, continuing photography of Japanese industrial targets, and with Black Dragon thugs continuing to harass me. Other times, I worked in the code room, was an interpreter for Ambassador Grew, and worked with Captain Morrison on various intelligence operations.

Okay, folks, I'll tell you. The War is over. We won. And it was many years ago. Our objective was to cultivate high-ranking Japanese officers and politicians and to turn them into spies for our side. We knew that it would be difficult to convince such officials with logic and bribes to betray their country because of their deeply engrained Bushido culture. Accordingly, we used all manner of dirty tricks. Blackmail was our favorite technique. We would inveigle the target into an untenable scenario— usually a comprising sexual encounter. Often, the female classmates of mine in that long-ago Japanese language class were our *femme fatales*. We had minimal success. (Note. Nowadays, the Soviet KGB uses this technique with females they dub "swallows.")

❅ ❅ ❅ ❅ ❅

"Marne, the National Command Authority is concerned. Generalissimo Chang Kai-shek's nationalist army is falling back on all fronts and the Empire's Kwangtung Army is advancing into the interior of China. At best, the Chinese are slowing the Japanese progress. And vast quantities of our aid has been sidelined into the pockets of leading Kuomintang officials."* (182)

"I understand, Captain Morrison."

"What I say next is classified Top Secret, Uranus. Only you and I are privy in this Embassy."

"Yes, sir."

"I have a communication from Mao Tse-tung,* (183) Chairman of the Central Executive Committee of the Chinese Communist Party, asking for military aid for his Eighth Route Army's guerilla war on the Japanese. How I got this message is irrelevant. What's relevant is Mao's request, and I have it."

Whoops! "Captain, we ought not to trust those Communist fellows. They are also fighting Chang's nationalist army and winning every battle. If we send weapons to Mao, the Communists will defeat Chang that much quicker."

Captain Morrison looked at me with a quizzical eye. "I'm hearing you say that, no matter what, Mao and his cadre will triumph and rule all China."

"Exactly. I am convinced that Communist rule is China's future."

"Maybe, Marne. Maybe. Nonetheless, ready for a trip to China?"

China? I've been to China. Thank you. With a touch of cheekiness in my voice, I replied, "Say again. Over."

I saw the captain wince slightly at my smart-ass remark. Nonetheless, he continued, "We are void of A1 intelligence on Mao's operations. That stuff we get from Chang's Ministry of State Security is propaganda and valueless."* He took a breath and continued *soto voce*. "Rear Admiral Walter Anderson* (184) has authorized a clandestine operation to meet with Chou En-lai.* (185) He's the Director of the Special Services Section of the Central Committee—its intelligence arm. Take the mettle of this man, negotiate, but promise nothing except to meet again after you get information from the State Department. Take your Leica. We've got twenty-five rolls of Eastman Kodak's new color film, Kodachrome.* (186) Supposed to be first class."

I had heard the Captain and my simple mind had processed his messages into coherent information. However, he had omitted a key element. "Pardon my temerity, Captain, but may I have permission to ask a relevant question, sir?"

"Marne, I tolerate your smart-ass attitude because you are worth keeping around. What do you want to know?"

"Is this a volunteer assignment?"

"No! You're it."

"Aye, aye, sir."

"Damn! You are indeed a classic smart ass."

"Indeed, Captain."

"Knock it off, Marne. There's more." Later, he smiled wickedly, patted me on the back, shook my hand, and said, "Godspeed."

No need to relay all the details. A few highlights will suffice. Our Air Operations Officer had planned our mission for the blackest night of the month. That morning, he filed our flight plan with the Japanese air traffic office. Our PBY Catalina was scheduled to fly east over the Pacific for ten hours on a practice rescue mission. Several hours before sunset, I boarded the Catalina at our dock in Tokyo Bay. I was wearing a Navy standard flight suit. Take-off and climb-out were smooth and uneventful. As expected, two Japanese Mitsubishi A6M Zero* navy fighters tailed us. About an hour out, we began practicing expanding square searches. Shortly, the Zeros returned to base.

Nine hours later we landed in a secluded cove in one of the small islands that dot the southern cost of Korea. The waist- and nose-gunners mounted their 50-caliber machine guns and charged the weapons with a round. Suddenly, several hundred yards to port, the sea roiled and white foam spilled off the deck of a surfacing submarine. Ours. With hand pumps, the refueling of the PBY took about thirty minutes.

So far, the Japanese had not spotted us. I can imagine their concern at headquarters about our whereabouts: crashed, decamped, or up to skull-duggery. Phone calls to the Embassy inquiring about our whereabouts were fielded by Captain Morrison. His answer was, "Our PBY seaplane had a slight engine problem. It has gone to Guam for repairs." Of course, the Japanese knew that he was lying. But that's the protocol of diplomacy, as it were.

We were airborne and flying almost due west. I changed into rough worker's clothing, and on my hip under the worn leather jacket was my 1911 Colt 45. I checked my official identification papers to ensure that I had my military identification card, official orders, and diplomatic documents as a member of the United States Embassy in Tokyo.

We penetrated the Japanese-occupied Chinese coast a few miles north of Tsingtao. We flew about ninety miles inside Shantung Province. No Japanese airplanes intercepted us. At the rendezvous point, I parachuted into the void, hit the ground hard, and tumbled catawampus—hurting my body all over. Folks, I must say that's a thrill for the record books. About thirty minutes later, a patrol of Eighth Army soldiers approached. I used my flashlight to give the recognition signal and they replied. So far, all was well.

Dawn was breaking and the lieutenant in charge led us to a cave in a karst knob about five kilometers away. We traveled at night for several days evading Japanese and Nationalist patrols. On the second night we almost stumbled into a Japanese division headquarters. Fortunately their guards didn't hear us. We circled around and pressed on. On the sixth night, we reached the village of Po-shan.

The Lieutenant said, "Mister Marne, we are here." He led me into a farmer's hut and pointed to the fellow and his wife. "These comrades will tend to you. Eat, drink fine water and green tea, and sleep. Your contact will arrive tomorrow." For a second or two, he stood at attention and snapped a salute, then he disappeared.

I drank and drank the delicious water, consumed a large bowl of rice and pork, and sipped a cup of green tea. Satiated, I collapsed on a cot strewn with straw and slept, dreaming of big, beautiful, brown eyes that smiled invitingly.

A tug on my left shoulder awakened me. It took a couple seconds for me to comprehend my surroundings and the squad of heavily-armed soldiers about me. I grabbed for my 1911 Colt 45. Gone. My Leica was on the floor beside the cot. One of the soldiers approached my cot. "Time to arise, Lieutenant Commander Marne, and join me for tea."

I rolled out of the cot, brushed the straw off my clothes, and with a wave of my right arm said in a too-loud voice, "And good morning to all of you fine fellows of the Eighth Route Army."

An officer approached and said in his official voice, "Permit me to introduce myself, I am Chou En-lai, Director of the Special Services Section of the Central Committee, Communist Party of China." We shook hands and he said, "Welcome to China. We shall have good fortune in our conversation." He made a subtle signal and a sergeant handed me my 1911 Colt 45. "Commander Marne, your pistol."

I took my weapon and noted that a loaded clip was in place. I stuck it in my belt holster. "Thank you, Comrade Chou. I look forward to understanding your concerns."

He sat at the table and beckoned me to join him. One of his lackeys poured the tea. (The farmer and his wife were not to be seen.) We spent the next thirty minutes in idle chit-chat, taking the mettle of each other. Chou was about five feet, seven inches tall. His body motion was smooth and confident. He was second only to Mao in the hierarchy of the Chinese Communist Party. He was handsome, courteous, keenly intelligent, and assured. With his approval, I snapped photographs of him, his cadre, and interiors of the hut.

During a break, Chou commented, "Lieutenant Commander Marne, I must tell you that, through a trusted intermediary, I asked your State Department's Bureau of Research and Intelligence for you by name."

Whoops! That's scary news. Nonetheless, it could be a positive. Let's see. "Comrade Chou, I am flattered that you know of me and have trusted me for this important meeting. Perhaps I may be of service."

For the record, folks, I do not cotton to the Leninist Communist political agenda. In fact, the whole Red kit and caboodle are Fascist squared. Nonetheless, I would work with this Red to explore his game plan.

Chou continued, "We have followed your career from your service on the *USS Panay*, suppression of warlords, and help with civilians escaping from Nanking. Your service to China is well documented in our comprehensive dossier. We knew you would be a professional without prejudice in this meeting."

Folks, how about that? I'm a minor hero, or 'pigeon,' with these Red fellows.

We spent the day talking about the People's Party fight against the Japanese, their successes, losses, and serious casualties. Chou's appeal for American modern arms, communication equipment, and medical supplies was reasoned and compelling. To maintain cordial relations, I did not mention their conflict with Chang's nationalists. About every hour we took a short walk. His soldiers were on guard in tactical positions. I made copious notes, replied courteously, snapped photographs, and was noncommittal. From time to time, I asked direct questions about his intelligence organization and operations: communications capability, training, agent deployment, and the like. Much to my surprise, he answered every question forthrightly. No denials. No gobbledygook. No filibustering. No changing the subject. His gambit to earn my trust.

Towards evening, he rose, and said, "I must leave now. My people will take you to your rendezvous near Tsingtao." As he shook my hand, he asked, "May I count on your support?"

"Comrade Chou, I am not empowered to make a commitment for my government. However, you may be assured that I will present your case for American arms forthrightly to appropriate United States officials." We shook hands, and I bade him, "Be well." Without ado, he was gone.

Folks, may I suggest that you read about Chou's career and his untimely death in January 1976. Had he lived to replace the seriously ill Mao Tse-tung, the history of the Far East might well have had a more peaceful narrative.

The lieutenant said, "We go now."

Five cautious nights later, we were at a dock in a small village north of Tsingtao. Standing by was a fifteen-foot boat with an outboard motor. At 0130 hours, I flashed my light in the appropriate identification signal towards the open sea. No response. Ten minutes later, ditto and ditto. At 0147 hours, a light coming from the sea flashed the correct identification signal. I replied, and immediately got the acknowledgement.

That outboard motor kicked to life, and I was en route to my ride to friendly environs. About five minutes later, a powerful searchlight lit our boat and a motor torpedo boat began to close quickly. Japanese, no doubt.* (187) Their machine gun began firing and bullets ripped into water close aboard and onto the boat. I hit the bottom of our boat *muy pronto.* And fortuitous it was. All of my Red escorts were hit, and the boat began circling uncontrollably. From the dark sea came the *rat-tat-tat, rat-tat-tat* of a pair of 50-caliber machine guns. The Japanese motor torpedo boat exploded in a mass of flames. The *deus ex machina* had arrived in the nick of time, dressed in pitch black: the submarine *USS S16.* * (188)

I debarked at our naval base in Guam. There was no way that submarine was going to sail into Tokyo Bay to put me ashore. A couple of days later, dressed in a new business suit courtesy of the U.S. Navy, I boarded the

Pan American China Clipper bound for Manila and Hong Kong. I spent four nights at the Peninsula Hotel to recoup and work on my report.* (189) British Overseas Airways to Tokyo and rickshaw to the Embassy.* (190)

Ditto the debriefing and report preparation, as with my Nomonhon episode. We sent the exposed Kodachrome to Naval Intelligence Headquarters in the diplomatic pouch for forwarding to the Eastman Kodak Company in Rochester for processing.* (191) Only place this type of film could be processed.

TWENTY-TWO

American Embassy, Tokyo, December 1941

At exactly 0253 hours on 8 December 1941, the Kenpeitai shattered the front door of the United States Embassy in Tokyo.* (192) They spilled inside with guns drawn and quickly had full control. The two Marines on watch, obeying Ambassador Crew's order, surrendered their arms.

Japanese naval aircraft had attacked our battle fleet at anchor in Pearl Harbor.* (193) It was 0753 hours on a Sunday morning, 7 December 1941. They sank five ships of the line,* (194) damaged several others, and wreaked havoc on military facilities. Two thousand and three hundred servicemen lost their lives in this dastardly attack.* (195) On 9 December, at a joint session of Congress, President Roosevelt asked for a declaration of war with the Empire of Japan.* (196)

Several weeks earlier, we had known to an absolutely certainty that war with Japan was imminent, and we had expected this smash occupation of our embassy. Accordingly, we had loaded our diplomatic pouches with the most relevant documents, valuable paintings, and other important stuff. My 1911 Colt 45 was included. It all headed to the Director of Naval Intelligence headquarters. A work party loaded the pouches on our PBY amphibian, and it broke water in Tokyo Bay headed for Guam.

Systematically, we had burned all other documents, and destroyed any equipment of value. We had transferred Captain Morrison and all our Q personnel to Corregidor in the Philippines via chartered Pan American World Airways. All but the three senior State Department officials remained. The Marine guards, all our civilian employees, and all dependents had been sent to Pearl Harbor, again via Pan American charters. The Kenpeitai had watched diligently, and took photographs of our comings and goings. However, they had not interfered.

I had remained as the Ambassador's aide de camp. The Embassy was empty and our footsteps on the marble floors sounded hollow and reverberated. Missed the most, I reckon, was our chef and his staff. On reflection, it was our butler. A 'cumshaw' artist of high order.

Over the past few days, I had visited on "official business" the British, Vichy French, Netherlands, and Portuguese embassies, and 'passed the word.' The British MI6 folks had been far ahead of me on Japanese intelligence—as usual.

A senior Japanese officer from the Ministry of Foreign Affairs entered our embassy. He did not introduce himself. He was dressed in a morning coat, black striped trousers, black shoes, and black top hat. Ambassador Grew, in a business suit, had been in the vestibule expecting his arrival. I wore my dress blues with medals and stood slightly behind and to the right of the ambassador.

The ministry officer bowed two times, looked Ambassador Grew in the eyes, and began, "Excellency, I have the privilege of delivering this Demarché from Shigenori Togo, Minister of Foreign Affairs.* (196A) I have the honor to inform Your Excellency that there has arisen a state of war between Your Excellency's country and the Empire of Japan beginning today. I avail myself of this opportunity to renew to Your Excellency the assurances of my highest consideration."

Folks, that paragraph above is a quote.

Obviously slightly chagrined, he continued, "Ambassador Grew, you and your staff are under Minister Shigenori Togo's protection. I will tell you that this morning our navy airplanes attacked Pearl Harbor and sank the United States Navy's battle fleet.. We expect a quick victory over your imperialist nation."

Several Kenpeitai soldiers approached and started to handcuff us. The ministry fellow snapped, "Not necessary." He shooed the Kenpeitai away and said, "Excellency, please follow me to the waiting limousine."

The entire embassy staff, all six of us, left the last vestige of the United States in the Land of the Rising Sun. We were taken to the Imperial Hotel* (197) in the Chiyoda Ward. Like any ordinary criminals, we had our mug shots and fingerprints taken, and sundry questions asked. Each of us responded in turn, "We are members of the United Sates Embassy and have diplomatic immunity."

The Foreign Affairs fellow responded, "It is true. We ask this information to notify the Scandinavian Legation of your particulars so that they might contact your State Department and communicate your whereabouts and well-being."

Ambassador Grew responded at first with just the minimum of information.

The fellow said, "You are interned in the Imperial Hotel as guests of the Empire of Japan. Each has a private room with bath. You may wander about the hotel as you wish. Visit the bar, dining room, shops, lobby, and the gardens. But, under no condition are you to use the outside telephone or leave the hotel. If so, you forfeit your diplomatic immunity. The Ministry will not be responsible for the untoward consequences resulting. Meantime, our ministry staff shall make arrangements for your repatriation via the *charge d' affaires* of the Scandinavian Legation." He started to leave but stopped in mid-stride. "Perhaps I should mention that this hotel was designed in 1926 by the famous American architect Mister Frank Lloyd Wright.* (198) It is beautiful, is it not?"

Ambassador Grew had a large suite and I had an adjoining mini suite. We were comfortable and safe—for now. The hotel staff performed remarkably well, catering to our every whim. I chuckled silently that the Empire of Japan was paying for my imbibing of Kentucky's finest. I spent my time walking in the garden, reading, chatting with Ambassador Grew and our other personnel. Visiting the venerable Old Imperial Bar* (199) on the second deck, overlooking the spacious lobby.

Over the next few weeks, diplomats, journalists, businessmen, dependents, and other Occidental nationals that the Ministry of Foreign Affairs had selected for repatriation flooded the hotel. The place was crowded and noisy. Folks nattering about when would they be repatriated, by what means, and what's happening in the war? Our world was the Imperial Hotel—nothing more.

Occasionally, a Foreign Ministry person would leave leaflets containing war news. They were propaganda extolling the Japanese conquest of Wake, Guam, Manila, Hong Kong, Malaya, Singapore, Burma, Siam, Sarawak, Brunei, North Borneo, the Dutch East Indies, and Papua, New Guinea.* (200) Our morale fell precipitously.

Sending our morale plummeting farther was news of the sinking of our heavy cruiser *USS Houston** (201) and aircraft carrier *USS Langley** (202) in the Java Sea, the British battleship *HMS Prince of Wales,** (203) and the battle-cruiser *HMS Repulse** (204) off the coast of Malaya. We were losing the war. Where was that *deus ex machina* when we needed it so desperately? No show!

Late on the afternoon of 2 February, our foreign minister liaison entered and contacted Ambassador Grew. After the formal folderol he said, "Your Excellency, I speak to you today as the Occidentals' senior diplomat. Please to inform the internees that arrangements have been concluded with the Swedish government for your repatriation. Tomorrow at noon, buses will take all the internees to the Swedish passenger ship *MS Gripsholm.** (205) The Swedish government has formally notified all warring powers of its schedule and route for its upcoming voyage with Occidental repatriates. Swedish officials onboard the *MS Gripsholm* will communicate details of the voyage after the ship clears Japanese waters."

I stood next to Grew and saw him crack a small smile. He asked, with a straight face, "What are the Japanese protocols?"

"All must be ready to depart exactly at noon. Assemble in lobby. Two suitcases only. Go to designated bus when name is called. No speaking until in berth aboard ship. You are the spokesman for all. The Kenpeitai is in charge of this operation. Obey all instructions faithfully and promptly. Failure to obey will result in dire consequences."

"I understand."

The fellow bowed several times, did an imperfect about-face, and departed forthwith.

"Marne, get our people organized for a meeting and start passing the word."

"Aye, aye, sir."

Folks, no need to relay the boring details of our sea journey to home waters; a few highlights ought to do. The *MS Gripsholm,* instead of the luxury liner it had once been, was now more of a troop ship. Notwithstanding the Swedish government's preparations with warring and neutral governments, our fear of submarine or sea-raider attack was constant. Occasionally, warplanes of various nations overflew the ship, and from time to time we spotted a warship. Once, a Japanese destroyer shadowed us for about 36 hours. Purpose unknown. Protection? Maybe. And maybe not.

We stopped in Japanese-occupied Singapore for fueling with bunker oil and loading of fresh vegetables, and to board several neutral businessmen and students. The operation was routine and within five hours we were sailing in the Malacca Strait headed for the Indian Ocean. Again warplanes overflew us. Japanese for sure. On our second day in the Indian Ocean, the Australian destroyer *HMAS Arunta** (206) came along our port side. The Aussie crew "manned the rails" in their dress-white uniforms in a formal naval salute.* (207) We crowded the *Gripsholm's* rails and shouted and cheered, and a young woman waved the American flag. The *Arunta* blew its horn several times and fell in trail. She followed us for several days and then one morning she was gone.

After 21 days at sea, the *Gripsholm* docked in Lourenco Marques in Portuguese Mozambique. The steward announced over the intercommunication system, "We will be in port for about twelve hours to take on bunker oil and supplies. You may go ashore. Attention, please. When this ship is prepared to depart, our steam horn will blow four blasts. Fifteen minutes later, we'll cast off the lines and be underway. Return promptly or be left behind."

Amazing how well it felt to forgo my sea legs and walk on terra firma. I wandered about the place. Snapped a few photographs. Wandered into the Polana Serena hotel's bar to sample the famous Portuguese port wine.* (207A) The place was crowded with subjects of King George imbibing the Brits' favorite fruit of the vine.* (208) I spotted a number of the Latin Americans sipping the wine and chatting lightheartedly. The diplomat from Chile beckoned me to his table. "Please join us, Mister Marne. You have met my wife, I recall, *Señora Angela Leticia.*"

I made a short bow from the waist. "*Señora, mucho gusto.*" She smiled faintly and did not offer her hand.

"And this is my daughter, *Señorita Karina Costanzia.*"

I repeated my bow. "*Estoy encantado de conocerte.*" (I'm glad to meet you.)

She rose and extended her hand. Long, carefully manicured fingers gripped my right hand sensuously. "And I am pleased to know you, Lieutenant Commander Marne. I've seen you several times about the ship, but did not make an opportunity to introduce myself. Sit next to me and please speak in English. I need the practice."

Señora Leticia's cheeks flushed at her daughter's breach of formal Spanish customs. I saw that she started to speak, then thought that a comment would be inappropriate in the company of an *Americano.*

Folks, let's pause in this narrative. Over the years, I've been in the company of some engagingly attractive females, but I must say that *Señorita Costanzia* was at the top of the list. She was gracefully tall; her face would launch a thousand ships; her light brown skin shone in the afternoon light; carefully brushed, dark-brown hair cascaded over her shoulders; and her eyes—those big, bright, brown eyes radiating sensuality—enchanted me. And, not to be indelicate, but her body was sculptured by a master—and she knew it.

With appropriate comments, I slid into the booth next to her. Not too close, mind you. Our badinage was lively and intelligent. Soon, I realized that she had moved ever so imperceptibly closer that our *derrieres* were touching. I smiled with slight embarrassment and started to ease away.

She noticed, and her right arm touched my shoulder. "Tell me of some of your adventures in the Orient."

No need to develop this scenario further. Was it a shipboard romance with enduring possibilities? Maybe. But on reflection, I reckon not. It was something more fundamental.

✳ ✳ ✳ ✳ ✳

The *Gripsholm* pitched and rolled in gale winds and rough seas as we sailed around Cape Horn. The dining room was uncrowded, as most passengers abandoned meals for a day or two. Food, such as it was, was served in disposable cups, as it was impossible for tableware to remain in place. A day or two later, the seas calmed and the passengers returned to the daily shipboard routines. A few shipboard romances blossomed and quickly faded.

✳ ✳ ✳ ✳ ✳

It was mid-morning, and the Atlantic air was nippy. The sky was clear and the sea moderately calm. I was walking on the promenade deck to loosen my joints. Greeted a few newfound friends and was in fine spirits—New York was only a week away. On my third roundtrip, I saw passengers crowding the port rail and pointing to an object in the sea. I used my binoculars and spotted a German submarine at about 700 yards.* (209) It was on the surface charging its batteries and the crew were exercising. *Would the captain honor diplomatic protocols?* was the murmur heard throughout the passengers. Surprisingly, the U-boat skipper ordered the deck bosun to dip its ensign to render honors to the returnees aboard the *Gripsholm.*

Suddenly, an overwhelming roar penetrated the air and a British Short Sunderland seaplane* (210) of the Royal Naval Air Service zoomed close to the U-boat. The waist gunner opened fire with his twin Browning 303 machine guns* (211) and I saw several German sailors fall into the sea.

The *Gripsholm's* captain gave the orders "Hard to starboard. Full speed ahead." The lee helmsman responded, "Full speed ahead," and pushed the brass handle of the engine order telegraph to its stop. The *Gripsholm* began to curve away from the action to port.

Meanwhile, the U-boat had cleared the deck and began its emergency dive. On its next pass, the Sunderland dropped two five-hundred-pound bombs. They straddled the diving U-boat in a blasting roar of fire and gushing water. The bow of the German U-boat leaped out of the sea, held its position for a few seconds, and then slid stern first into Davy Jones locker—all hands lost. No need to search for survivors. The Sunderland flew close aboard on our port side, dipped its wing in salute, gained altitude, and disappeared.

Imagining that submarine drowning in the sea with its crew of able seaman engendered an intense sorrow that gripped my soul. I had a choke in my throat. Enemy combatants indeed, but nonetheless a terrible waste. I note, dear reader, that all the passengers who witnessed this mass death of the German sailors remained mute. I left the rail to reduce the bar's stock of Kentucky's finest.

❋ ❋ ❋ ❋ ❋

We had docked at Ponta Delgada in the Portuguese Azores to debark the European passengers and to refuel and resupply fresh foodstuffs. The rest of us were restricted to the ship. The *polícia* guided the Europeans to the gangplank of the *MS Serpa Pinto** (212) of the Portuguese *Companhia.* She was bound for the port in Lisbon.

I had remained in my cabin and was reading a novel of no import. I responded to a rap on my door. It was the second officer and a tall fellow in mufti. The fellow entered my cabin uninvited, closed the door, no introduction, and flashed a badge of some sort. "Lieutenant Commander Marne, pack your gear and follow me. We're late. Questions later. We have to leave this ship now to meet a closing schedule."

I'd been in this man's Navy long enough to understand the essence of this unfolding scenario. Ten minutes later we were walking down the gangplank. We piled into a waiting sedan that drove us to a secluded cove a mile or two from the ship's port. No secret, now. I spotted the Pan American World Airways Boeing B-314 seaplane "Yankee Clipper" at anchor. The fellow finally spoke: "Let's move. That ship should have taken off several hours ago. Influential muck mucks have ordered it held until you were aboard."

The instant I fastened my seatbelt, I heard the number three engine cough twice and roar to life. Within a minute all four engines were alive and throbbing in a steady, rhythmic beat. The dock handlers cast off the bow and stern lines, and the captain eased the throttles forward. He deftly maneuvered the giant Pan American World Airways Boeing flying boat into the main channel. The skipper completed the check list, got the "thumbs up" from the flight engineer, and advanced the throttles. The Boeing flying boat's four Wright R-2600, radial, 1,600 horsepower engines each roared thunderously, and the *Yankee Clipper* skimmed the placid waters, leaving a whale-like rooster tail. Forty-five seconds later, the flying boat broke the suction holding it to the sea and was airborne. Foamy water streamed off its hull.

There were no questions and therefore no answers. Nonetheless, in effect, I was shanghaied off the *Gripsholm* 'cause some grand poohbah reckoned that I was a valuable asset and was needed in Washington, D.C. post haste. Beats me. Ambassador Grew must have known more than I.

Twelve hours later, the *Yankee Clipper* landed in Long Island Sound and moved to the bay at the LaGuardia Marine Air Terminal. I was almost the last passenger off the flying boat. Waiting for me on the dock were a senior lieutenant and a chief boatswain mate, both wearing a guard belt and leggings, with a Colt 45 in a holster attached to the guard belt. Whoops! This meant serious business.

The officer saluted. "Lieutenant Commander Marne, I am the duty officer at Naval Base Long Island. Welcome home."

I did not return the salute because I was in mufti. I responded, "Thanks. Why the garb and *pistoles?*" In a flash, I realized how stupid my comment was. We were at war. "Never mind. I understand."

"I have a sedan waiting for you. Let's get your gear."

"Lieutenant, everything I own is in this bag I'm carrying."

"The Director of Naval Intelligence, Rear Admiral Theodore Wilkinson.* (213) is expecting you in Washington soonest. We have a PBY Catalina standing by."

Folks, this scenario was getting too deep for my simple mind. I was a mid-level naval officer. Other folks in this Navy knew one hell of a lot more about the war than I. I had been incommunicado for almost four months. All I knew was what the Kenpeitai had told us. And most of that was garbage. Onboard the *Gripsholm,* the scant war news we had learned, via the ship's daily bulletin, was that the Japanese were winning the war. It was true.

❉ ❉ ❉ ❉ ❉

The admiral's staff intelligence officer, Captain Timothy Kirchbaum, led my debriefing team—six days of talking with a cadre of navy and civilian intelligence types and being mentally manhandled by psychiatrists aplenty.

I had my naked body punched, pinched, and abused by a corps of so-called medical professionals with needles, tubes, bottles, bags of various sizes and configuration, and large and small machines that go "Zip-a-dee-doo-dah" or something. The medico found that I was somewhat malnourished and had a low-grade infection, its clinical name far beyond my skill level. The magic cure, I was led to believe, was a dose of the newfangled drug dubbed penicillin, inserted into my *derriere* by a frowning, sadistic nurse with a large "square" needle, and a bottle of tablets of the same name.

I recovered 27 rolls of 35mm black-and-white film from the attaché's diplomatic pouch. At least, the Japanese had honored diplomatic protocol. Several days later, the photographic laboratory had printed several hundred 8x10-inch prints. Captain Kirchbaum scanned the prints, and commented, "Marne, these photographs of yours are dynamite. Amazing! I'll send them to our targeting people for detailed evaluation and have those targets incorporated into the Bombing Encyclopedia and target folders. When we begin strategic bombing of the Japanese home islands, these images will augur well for precision targeting."

Reckon I erred: I knew lots more than I knew I knew. In my interview with Admiral Earnest King, USN, Chief of Naval Operations,* (214) he congratulated me for tasks well done, and awarded me the Bronze Star.* (215) Admiral King capped the interview by saying, "We hurried you here because we needed urgently both your information on your assignments in the Orient, and those dynamite targeting photographs. Lots happening, I can't discuss. You'll learn shortly. Also, Marne, I am sending you to Hawaii tomorrow. Fleet Admiral Chester Nimitz, USN, Commander-in-Chief Pacific Fleet,* (216) has requested you by name to be assigned to his headquarters staff at Makalapa, Pearl Harbor."

There went my plans for thirty-day leave, long overdue. But what the hell. There was a war on.

"Before I continue, I regret to tell you that Captain William Morrison was captured on Cavite and was killed during the Bataan Death March.* (217) Fortunately, our submarines have evacuated all "Q" personnel from Corregidor. Keep that information confidential."

"Aye, aye, sir." What is there to say about Captain Morrison? He was a fine naval officer and we'll miss him. This is going to be an unearthly episode in world history. *C'est la guerre.*

I began to leave. The Admiral said, "Lieutenant Command Marne, you've forgotten something." He opened a desk drawer, withdrew my 1911 Colt 45, and handed it to me. "Use this weapon wisely."

With a large smile, I commented, "Thanks for husbanding my Colt. Indeed, sir, I shall use it prudently."

TWENTY-THREE

CINCPACFLT Headquarters, Pearl Harbor, Territory of Hawaii,
March 1942

Because of my broad naval experiences and my so-called language skills, the staff intelligence officer appointed me the leader of a traffic-analysis team that monitored a myriad of Japanese naval messages. Our team was a part of Commander Joseph Rochford's* (218) "Station Hypo" operation—the Navy's top code-breaking outfit.

I had a great team: Lieutenant Charles Hayashi, a Nisei from Oakland and graduate of Stanford University with a doctorate in International Relations. The other officer was Ensign Bernardino (Dino) D'Angelo, a post-graduate student at the Massachusetts Institute of Technology studying quantum physics. My four enlisted ratings consisted of two "Q" senior petty officers and two WAVEs (Women Accepted for Voluntary Emergency Service* (219) in training for the "Q" rating.

Also, there were three civilians on my team: one was a senior mathematician from the University of Texas* (220), another was a champion chess player from back East someplace, and the third was a professor of philosophy from the University of Southern California.* (220A) To paraphrase Lord Tennyson, "I don't know the reason why, they did it. Do not pry."* (221)

The Japanese navy frequently changed its codes. With consummate skill, Rochford and his cryptographic "Q" gang would do their magic and peek inside the new codes, then crack them open.

The Doolittle Raid, April 1942

In February 1942, Lieutenant Colonel James (Jimmy) Doolittle* (222), aviation pioneer who had won the National Air Races in 1932 in a Gee Bee R1* (223), devised a daring surprise for the Empire of Japan. General George C. Marshall, Chairman of the Joint Chiefs of Staff,* (224) gave his approval. Training of volunteer aircrews began.

At station Hypo, we had back-channel updates on Doolittle's scheme. And we carefully screened Japanese message traffic to learn if they had an inkling of his surprise. Apparently not.

On the morning of 18 April, 1942, Doolittle led sixteen B25 Mitchell medium bombers from the flight deck of the aircraft carrier *USS Hornet** (225) (dubbed *Shangri-La* by the press)* (226) and bombed targets in Tokyo, Yokosuka, Nagoya, and Kobe. I understood the Navy's rush to get my targeting photographs.

This raid, the first on the Japanese archipelago, boosted the American psyche, which had been in the doldrums following the disaster at Pearl Harbor, our loss of Wake, Guam, and the Philippines, our defeat in the Battle of Java Sea, and Japan's overwhelming victories in Southeast Asia over our Occidental allies. Doolittle's surprise air raid seriously alarmed the Spirit Warriors in Tokyo—the white devils had violated the sacred land of the Chrysanthemum Throne. General Hideki Tojo, Minister for War,* (227) issued orders to various forward-deployed military resources to return to their bases. Those assets were now needed to protect the home islands.

Battle of Midway, 4 to 7 June 1942

In late April and early May 1941, Imperial Japanese Navy traffic increased to a roar, and it was in their new code, dubbed J25—a tiger to break. Suddenly, in late May, there was no message traffic. Nothing. Not a peep from Admiral Isoroku Yamamoto's* (228) Combined Fleet* (229). The Japanese airwaves were deadly silent. Clearly, Admiral Yamamoto was planning a major strike.

My traffic analysis team worked in concert with Commander Rochford's Q team, employing every cryptographic tactic we could imagine. No success. Every day that passed was critical, and our anxiety heightened. Admiral Nimitz gave us full support. We could see the strain in his face and stature. It appeared that we were facing another Pearl-Harbor-style attack and the resultant overwhelming Japanese success.

Sometimes, perhaps, we overlook the ingenuity of our men. One of the Q sailors devised a simple yet ingenious ruse that duped the Japanese into transmitting a message *en clair* that contained a key to their J25 naval code. The Rockford team cracked the code in due course.

(The details of this ruse are described in other publications.)

Admiral Yamamoto's combined fleet of five aircraft carriers, six battleships, a cadre of heavy and light cruisers, dozens of destroyers, troop transport ships, and support ships were underway for an invasion of Midway Atoll—only 1140 nautical miles from Pearl Harbor, and the last island in the Hawaiian chain. Admiral Yamamoto's invasion was scheduled for 4 June 1941.

Having this A1 intelligence, Admiral Nimitz planned an ambush with his two carriers, *USS Enterprise** (230) and *USS Yorktown.** (231)

The battle engaged on 4 June and by 7 June the American Navy had sunk four Japanese aircraft carriers and damaged a host of other vessels. We lost the *Yorktown.* Nonetheless, this overwhelming naval victory was the turning point of the Pacific War. Henceforth we were the aggressors and the Japanese were the defenders.

Guadalcanal, 7 August 1942 to February 1943

Our first major amphibious offensive on a Japanese-held island was in August 1942. The Fleet Marines of the First Division landed on Guadalcanal in the Japanese-occupied British Solomon Islands. The Marines quickly captured Henderson Air Field, and the Japanese fought doggedly to retake it.

I remember the day with precision. It was 30 September 1942, and I was standing at attention in Fleet Admiral Chester Nimitz's office.

"At ease, Marne." The admiral rose and went to a wall-size map of the Solomon Islands.* (232) He tapped a long pointer on one of the larger islands. "Commander Marne, our Marines and soldiers on Guadalcanal are catching Hell. Casualties are outrageously high. They captured Henderson Field in a couple of days. Now, those damn Japs are determined to recapture it and kick our fantails back into the Coral Sea. And the way the fighting is developing, they just might do it." He tapped his pointer on the map several times as his mind finessed the details. "Won't do. Won't do 't all."

Notes. It's navy the custom to address lieutenant commanders as "Commander." And for the record, Fleet Admiral Chester Nimitz was from Fredericksburg, Texas.

The Admiral continued tapping for a few seconds more. "Commander Marne, get your team and portable equipment assembled. Tomorrow you're going to Guadalcanal. Get Lieutenant General Vandergrift* (233) the tactical signal intelligence he needs to kick the Japs off this island. I'll have our Martin PBM Marnier standing by."* (234)

He handed me a small box. Inside were two silver oak leaves. I blinked twice as the reality of this early promotion to Commander penetrated my mind.* (235) Before I could comment, the admiral continued. "If you are to work directly with General Vandergrift and his colonel staff intelligence officer, you'll need to have more cachet. Don't want you bogged down in the bureaucracy of his staff. Shove off, Commander Marne."

"Aye, aye, admiral."

A few days later I was dressed in Marine fatigues (greens) with no insignia or rank symbols. Our quarters and work space were in a large tent on the south side of Henderson Field, secreted in a copse of palm trees—or what was left of them. I had my 1911 Colt 45 in a holster attached to my guard belt. Lieutenant Charles Hayashi and my two "Q" ratings, similarly armed, manipulated the intercept radio equipment. Each of us had the "pill" in a small, bright yellow box: We could not be captured; eventually, the Japanese would have garnered our country's innermost intelligence secrets. Outside the tent were two Marine guards with Tommy guns (Thompson 45 caliber submachine guns.)* (236)

We cracked the Japanese field codes *très vite.* Fortunately, many of the Japanese junior officers were sending much of their communication in a tactical code we cracked forthwith. Some emergency messages were transmitted *en clair.* In our first evening, we sent General Vandergrift's staff A1 intelligence on Japanese intentions, troop positions, supply stream, and more.

That night, forewarned, the Marines established an ambush for the expected Banzai charge. And so it went for several weeks. Now, the Marines were inflicting severe casualties on the Japanese, and the 'leathernecks' were gaining the tactical advantage.

Henderson Field was operating no matter the stray bullets whizzing by, errant motor shells dropping randomly, and occasional Japanese sniper pinging at everyone Twenty-four hours a day, a mélange of aircraft took off and landed: F3F Wildcats,* (237) F4U Corsairs,* (238) P38 Lightening,* (239) PBY Catalinas,* (240) almost any aircraft in our inventory—including an F2A Buffalo* (241) from the Royal Northlands Air Arm,* (241A) a survivor from their lost campaign in the Dutch East Indies.

The Japanese were exceptionally intelligent. One evening, in late November, a squad of Japanese marines hit our encampment. Our two Marine guards cut down most of the attackers. Nonetheless, each Marine fell with multiple wounds.

At the first sound of the Tommy-gun's chatter, I yelled, "Attack." Hayashi armed the destruction mechanism on our classified equipment and flipped the red switch. It evaporated in intense white flames. Japanese bullets ripped into our tent, and one "Q" rating fell. The 1911 Colt 45 was in my right hand. A Japanese marine stormed into our tent and lunged at me with his bayoneted rifle, screaming, "Banzai!" My Colt spoke volumes and the fellow had two large holes in his gut. Nonetheless, he pressed the attack and jammed his bayonet into my left side. As I fell, I gasped for breath and my thought was, "Gadzooks! Another Purple Heart."* (242)

I have faint mental images of Hayashi tending me. A corpsman administering sulfonamide or something. He stuck some tube down my throat, and that's all I remember.

❋ ❋ ❋ ❋ ❋

My first clear recollection was of a hospital room somewhere. It was gently rolling from side to side. It was riding the waves in the briny—*ergo*, a hospital ship. Which? Japanese? American? En route to where? The pain in my left side was intense. I used my right hand to rub it and felt a bundle of bandages. The Japanese bayonet, of course. I had tubes stuck in my nose and a machine that went "pocketa, pocketa, pocketa." What was that about? And there were all manner of tubes stuck in my arms leading to bottles of stuff, and a tube from my side.

The female in white at my bedside spoke in a soft voice. "Commander Matthew Marne, welcome aboard the *USS Solace*."* (243) She gave me her best personal smile. "I'm Lieutenant Maria Sanchez-Navarro and I'm the nurse who is taking care of you. And, I must tell you that I have the basic special intelligence clearance and so does your doctor, Captain Nectarous Jacomedies. The back channel will confirm. And that's why I'm your nurse, and no one else." With a devilish smile she said *soto voce*, "*¿Comprender? Commander Marne?*" With major difficulty, I managed to reply, "*De hecho entiendo, mi dama in blanco.*" (In fact, I understand, my lady in white.)

Nurse Sanchez-Navarro smiled softly and continued, "*Muy bien.*" She placed a thermometer under my tongue, and smiled coquettishly. "*Por favor, commandente, es señorita.*" (Please, Commander, I am a mistress.) She read the instrument. "To business: How are 'y'all' feeling?"

I muttered, "Lousy! The devil is dancing in my left inside. And what are these tubes stuck in my nose?"

"That Japanese bayonet jabbed your left lung. It collapsed. And you have an infection in the wound. Yesterday, Captain Doctor Jacomedies and our medical team performed surgery, and your prognosis is positive. We're injecting your fantail with shots of penicillin to kill that acute infection."

"I understand, I reckon." And damn! Another infection. "Pray tell, Nurse Maria, how close to the Pearly Gates was I?"

"Not sure. But the corpsman who saved you by applying artificial respiration implied that Saint Peter was just about to log you in."

"Do you have his name?"

"No, unfortunately. He continued until the medicos had you on a respirator." She adjusted a knob on some instrument. "*Suficiente.* Time for your pain shot. Give me your right arm palm up." She did the deed.

Nurse Maria was a tall, comely lass with sparkling, deep brown eyes, shiny light-brown hair, an oversupply of curves, long, shapely legs, and an 'attitude.' Reckon I was staring—unseemly, to be sure.

To quiet my questioning/lustful eyes, she said, "At ease, commander. I'm from Bandera in central Texas. And I see that you're from Marfa in west Texas. *Muy bien, mi compatriota.*" (Very good, my compatriot)

As I drifted to dreamland, I saw images of Maria and I on the quarterdeck. Bob Wills and his Light Crust Doughboys were playing Western music.* (244) We were dancing the "Cotton-eyed Joe," "Put Your Little Foot," and the two-step.

Next morning, Doctor Jacomedies and Nurse Sanchez-Navarro took my vital signs, changed the dressings, and applied some arcane pharmaceutical nostrums to fight that damn infection.

"Ready for your shot?"

"Damn right, some phantom has ignited a fire in that wound."

Nurse Sanchez-Navarro did the deed.

Before I drifted away, I asked, "Any word on my crew? How long have I been here? Where are we bound?"

Nurse Sanchez-Navarro replied, "Commander, too many questions. All will be answered in due time. For now, we're bound for the Navy Hospital on Espiritu Santo in the British Protectorate New Hebrides."

This time I dreamed of the beautiful Veronica, a Marine campaign hat, and that Chinese 3¢ surcharge on that red revenue stamp.

Several weeks later, I learned that Hayashi and I were the only survivors from our intelligence tent on Guadalcanal. God! This is a rotten business.

Note. The Marines secured Guadalcanal in February 1943.

Other than a Japanese submarine alert about two days out, nothing of significance happened. Our escorting destroyer shooed it away with a brace of depth bombs. Nurse Sanchez-Navarro's care was keenly professional and had a deft personal touch. Her ready smile and cheerful voice eased the stultifying tedium. I had no challenges. Nothing to do. I was bored. She was my contact with the world. From time to time, Maria and I flirted a tad, with *bon mots*, and *double entendre*—of no import, mind you. Frankly, I was attracted to this beauty in white who stirred my soul. Was it lust, something more serious, or some combination of both? I was smitten.

A day out from Espiritu Santo, Maria bounced into my room. She was all smiles. "*Commandente, mi amigo*, I have a surprise for you."

I don't like surprises; nonetheless, let's see what she has planned.

She spotted the slight frown on my forehead.

She closed the door. "Matthew, you will like my surprise, I assure you." She placed a small box on the side table and started to unbutton her nurse uniform. She stopped at her waist. "Damn, it's warm in here. Close your eyes, Commander, and let me develop this scene."

I felt her face close to mine and detected her faint aroma. I heard her rumbling around, and my imagination painted several erotic scenarios.

"Open up, big boy."

I did.

Her uniform was fully buttoned, and a document of some sort was in her left hand. In her right hand was a military medal. She leaned close to me and pinned the Silver Star on my robe.* (245) She kissed me full on the lips. "*Mi héroe, Commandente*. Your award arrived today via highline from the supply ship. Fleet Admiral Nimitz sends you his congratulations."

Maria. This woman had enchanted my being.

✳ ✳ ✳ ✳ ✳

I was not ambulatory on arrival at Espiritu Santo, but under Maria's careful supervision, I was transferred from the *Solace* to the naval hospital. Folks that was an experience for the sinners in Hades. Nonetheless, my hospital room was bright, and from the window I could see a classic South Sea island scene: palm trees and gentle breakers on a white sandy beach. No scantily clad females dancing to welcome me, however.

Maria had ensured that every detail of the transfer to my room met her approval. She shooed away the orderlies and unpacked my duffle, storing the items with meticulous care. She withdrew my 1911 Colt 45 semi-automatic pistol. She inspected it, seemingly with a knowing eye.

"Cowboy, what are you doing with this cannon?" Before I could respond, she dropped the clip, ejected the round in the chamber, and field-stripped the thing faster than I could. "Nice weapon. Kind'a old. Any good?"

"Saved my life a couple of times."

"*Bueno.*" She re-assembled my Colt and handed it to me. "I'll keep the 45 round as a memento."

"Sure, keep it. Where did you learn about Colt 45s?"

"I live on a ranch in the Hill Country, on the old Gregory grant, and the diamondback are a damn nuisance—that is, until I blow their heads off with my Colt 45."

She tackled the adjustments on my bed, manipulating levers, cranks, and pedals until she was satisfied that I was comfortable. Once I was ensconced and "comfortable" in my new bed, she took my right hand, and with a choke in her voice said, "*¿Cómo te sientes, mi compadre?*" (How do you feel, my friend?)

"*Estoy bien.* Many thanks, sweet Maria, for your tender care. I shall remember you and will be always grateful."

We heard the steam horn on the *Solace* blow five short blasts and one long blast—fifteen minutes to sailing. Soft tears trickled down Maria's cheeks. "*Adios, mi compadre.*" She brushed my cheek with her wet lips, and moved her hand over the bandages on my wound. She stood tall, and said in full voice, "Commander Mathew Marne, I could love you." Her voice faltered but she continued, "Love you with all my heart and soul." Now, with tears streaming down her cheeks, she took my right hand and pressed it to her cheek. After a moment, she asked in a tender voice, "Matthew Marne, will you marry me—after the war?" Sobs racked her being and she dashed out of the room and ran down the passageway.

Folks, I have to tell you, I never saw Maria again. There were no letters, no telegrams, and no telephone calls. A shipboard romance, perchance?

The medical team at the Navy hospital on Espiritu Santo was first class and I recovered apace. Finally, in mid-February 1943, the medicos discharged me with the proviso that I be assigned to light duty only, and that I use a cane to ease the strain on the wound.

Awaiting orders, I milled about smartly in the Bachelor Officers' Quarters and in the Officer's Club making a nuisance of myself. Finally, late in the month, a seaman from the Communication Center gave me a Priority message. It was from CINCPACFLT. Fleet Admiral Nimitz was sending a VIP-configured PBM Marnier for transport to Pearl Harbor, to arrive 1 March 43. Then, that was it. I headed for Makalapa and the Green Door.

❋ ❋ ❋ ❋ ❋

Alright, I will tell you. You'll find out anyhow. Might as well get it straight from me. As I recall, it was about 15 November 1943. I received a letter postmarked 2 October 1943, Bandera, Texas. It had followed me across the central Pacific. Pedro Sanchez-Navarro wrote, "Maria, my only daughter, spoke of you often in her letters. I'm sure that she loved you deeply. And I am confident that you shared her love and had planned a life together after the war.

Maria was assigned to the Australian *Hospital Ship Centaur* in an exchange program.* (246) It was the night of May 14, 1943, and the *Centaur* was sailing off the coast of Queensland near Rackham, en route to Brisbane to debark wounded ANZAC troops from New Guinea. A Japanese submarine torpedoed the *Centaur*. This hospital ship exploded and sank almost immediately with nearly all hands. The Navy's Bureau of Personnel telegram said, 'Lieutenant Maria Sanchez-Navarro, United States Reserve, was lost at sea.' They sent me her Purple Heart medal and a folded American flag. Please to pray for her soul. I would be most pleased if you would come to Bandera after the war. I wish to meet you and hear your stories about *mi hijita*. I have asked God to look over you and keep you from harm."

TWENTY-FOUR

*CINCPACFLT Headquarters, Pearl Harbor, Territory of Hawaii,
February 1943*

On arrival at Makalapa, Fleet Admiral Nimitz said, "Welcome aboard, Commander Marne. Delighted that you're with us again. We'll find some interesting things for you to work on while you gain full strength and mobility."

"Thank you, sir."

For the next few months, I worked on the admiral's various intelligence assignments: Japanese Order of Battle, fleet deployments, and decoding the messages from our assets inside the Empire of Japan, the young female Nisei, as it were. Based on my background, my task was to evaluate their information for accuracy and credibility. We rated the reliability of each source from A (complete reliability) to E (invalid information). Information content was rated from 1 (confirmed) to 5 (improbable). When I reckoned the information was rated at least B2, I valued it as intelligence, marked its rating, incorporated it into our database, and sent it to appropriate organizations and individuals classified in the SCI system. And, yes, we did have protocols to detect double agents, ruses, or other interference in the messages.

By December 1943, it was crystal clear that, at long last, we were winning the war. I'd not had leave for six years, and I was mentally and physically exhausted. The admiral signed my thirty-day-leave slip and gave me orders for A1 priority on military flights.

Mom and dad had died while I was in the central Pacific. I missed their funerals. Cousins and nephews made the funeral arrangements.

Our homestead in Marfa was closed. For reasons I don't recall, I had not given a General Power of Attorney to any of my relatives. Should have. Reckon I wanted to take care of things my way. Fortunately, mom and dad had a will and I was named executor and beneficiary. I hired two maids and repairmen to get the family home in shipshape. In three days. All was well. I did not do anything for several days: read, slept, and ate junk food. Snow was on the ground and it was cold in this mountain community. I walked about my place and the town, and I was bored. Got my flivver out of storage, tinkered with it for a couple of days. I had transportation and even had a gasoline ration book with a "B" sticker, entitled to eight gallons of petrol a week. I visited old haunts.

The war had changed Marfa dramatically: there was a huge Army Air Corps base just south of town and airmen flooded the area. There were new buildings, new people; my sleepy west Texas town was booming in a temporary economy.

I tried to find some hunting companions. No deal. All my ol' pals were in the service—a few would not return. By accident (if you believe that, I have a bridge in Brooklyn for sale), I discovered that Eugenia was fine and had a son, and that her husband had serious heart problems. I started to make a call to the Pinto Canyon Ranch. However, a few miles down the road I turned around and headed home—reckoned it was not appropriate.

I made a telephone call to the central operator in Bandera, and asked to be connected to Mister Sanchez-Navarro.

She said, "I'm sorry to tell you that my second cousin, Pedro, died several months ago, and his wife has moved to Fort Worth. I have no forwarding information. It was very sad." She continued, "A diamondback struck Pedro in his chest while he was working in his Victory Garden, and his weak heart could not endure the strain. May I connect you to someone else?"

"Thank you, no."

I took the Southern Pacific train *Sunset Limited* to visit the "big city," San Antonio. Stayed at the St. Anthony Hotel,* (247) visited the Alamo,* (248) sipped a brew in the Menger Hotel bar,* (249) visited the Mission

San Jose,* (250) and photographed its Rose Window.* (251) That evening, I ate dinner in the Anacacho Room* (251A) at the hotel, and the big band played popular Tin Pan Alley tunes. Danced with several unaccompanied females, nice but of no import. Slept deeply. Next morning, at breakfast, I realized that I was bored. My shipmates were fighting for their lives.

❋ ❋ ❋ ❋ ❋

"Marne, you're early." The admiral had spotted me walking toward my desk.

"Sir, I was bored and I had to rejoin the war."

"I hear you. I'll work the problem."

For the next several months, I resumed my duties. My prime focus was on the communications from our Nisei females in-country. (Folks, to this day their transmission method remains classified.) Over the next few months, their information became scarce and unreliable. Concerned, the admiral, staff intelligence office, Commander Rochford, and I conferred behind the green door and we concluded that all or most all of our female Nisei agents had been compromised. The Kenpeitai were experts in coun-terintelligence. Naval intelligence had several "sleeper" agents in-country still asleep. Our dilemma was, should we activate one to investigate the whereabouts of our female agents? We needed approval from the director of naval intelligence before we could exercise such a delicate operation. Because of the extreme sensitivity of our inquiry, the admiral said, "No message. Commander Marne, you're it. Talk with the director and send us a message either 'yes' or 'no,' nothing else. Our BPM will take you to Oakland."

No need to relay the details. In summary, the Director of Naval Intelligence, Rear Admiral Roscoe E. Schuirmann,* (252) said, "Not now."

❋ ❋ ❋ ❋ ❋

It was a sunny morning in August 1944. I was standing at attention in Fleet Admiral Chester Nimitz's office. "At ease, Commander Marne. You need sea duty to hone your tactical intelligence and management skills. I have an assignment for you that will challenge you full-time. I've signed orders for you to report to Admiral William Halsey,* (253) Commander of the Third Fleet, onboard his flagship, the *USS New Jersey.** (254) You will be his staff intelligence officer." The admiral shook my hand. "I have every confidence that you will do your best."

"Thank you, admiral. It's the kind of assignment I was counting on."

He approached and handed me a small box. Inside was a pair of eagle collar devices. Stunned, I stumbled, "Sir? I'm not in the promotion zone. Far from it."

"Congratulations, Captain Matthew Marne.* (255) That Third Fleet staff intelligence job is a captain's billet." He shook my hand again and said, "Well deserved, our *Panay* radioman. We'll miss you. Godspeed." After a moment, he continued. "Now, the *New Jersey* is in our fleet anchorage in the Ulithi Atoll in the Carolines.* (256) I'll have our PBM take you."

Folks, please note. In October 1944, the Third Fleet was composed of 8 Fleet Carriers with about 640 aircraft, 8 Light Carriers with about 200 aircraft, 6 Battleships, 6 Heavy Cruisers, 9 Light Cruisers, 58 Destroyers, 23 Submarines, and various support ships.

TWENTY-FIVE

Aboard the USS New Jersey, Ulithi Atoll, Caroline Islands,
August 1944

Admiral Halsey greeted me, "Welcome to the Third Fleet Staff, Captain Marne. Lots happening in the central Pacific soon. Get updated. I'm counting on you to keep me informed with precision intelligence."

"Admiral, will do—count on it."

The *New Jersey* ship's company intelligence team was singularly competent—well-rounded in broad-based skills. The "happening" was that in mid-October, General Douglas MacArthur* (257) would begin the liberation of the Philippines. He would land a hundred thousand troops on Leyte,* (258) determined to fulfill his promise to the citizens of that archipelago: "I shall return."

And he did. At dawn on 20 October 1944, elements of the Sixth Army invaded Leyte. By early afternoon, they had secured the beach and territory several miles inland, making it safe enough for General of the Army General Douglas MacArthur to wade through the surf to shore.* (259)

No need to recount the army's battle ashore. It has been documented elsewhere. What was critical was the Imperial Japanese Navy's desperate, almost suicidal, sortie to save their key lifeline to the riches of Southeast Asia. Perhaps the greatest sea battle of all time, the Battle of Leyte Gulf, began on 23 October and ended on 26 October. The U.S. Navy's Third and Seventh Fleets engaged the Japanese armada, resulting in its total defeat. Details of this monumental sea battle are far too complicated to recount here.

Station Hypo had broken most of the Imperial Japanese naval codes. Accordingly, naval intelligence knew most of the details of the Japanese battle plan, but not all. Admiral Halsey's Third Fleet had been assigned to protect the landing on Leyte and the support ship in the gulf. On the 23rd, we were engaged with a large contingent of Japanese warships in surface action, and were defending the fleet from attacking Japanese aircraft based on Luzon. Late in the afternoon of 24 October, one of our patrol aircraft spotted a large Japanese carrier force steaming northward, away from Leyte Gulf.

With trepidation, I handed Admiral Halsey the message. He read it carefully. Folded it and jammed it in his breast pocket. He looked at me with those devilish eyes, and with glee in his voice boasted, "About time. I've been searching for Vice Admiral Ozawa's fleet* (260) for months. Now, we got him. I'm going after that bastard and sink him and his fleet to Hell."

"Sir, I have A-3 intelligence that suggests that this Japanese large carrier group is a decoy to lure the Third Fleet away from Leyte Gulf."

Halsey looked at me as if I were senseless. "What are you saying, Marne? Those four carriers and two battleships are valuable targets. Here is a golden opportunity to annihilate the Imperial Japanese Navy's last few remaining carriers."

"Admiral, indeed, you are correct. Nonetheless, I must caution you that those Japanese ships are some of the oldest in their fleet and the aerial photography shows that there are only about one hundred aircraft aboard those carriers. And it is not the main Japanese fleet—now steaming toward the San Bernardino Strait."

"Captain Marne, I hear you. I am ordering the Third Fleet to pursue and engage Vice Admiral Ozawa's fleet."

His nickname, "Bull," was appropriate. I knew he was making the most grievous error. "Admiral Halsey, sir, I must caution you not to succumb to this tempting Japanese ruse."

I pointed to Leyte Gulf on our situation map, and said, now with a greater sense of urgency, "Admiral, I have A-1 intelligence that Admiral Kurita's center fleet is now approaching the San Bernardino Strait. Without the Third Fleet as a blocking force, the landing at Leyte and those few light carriers, destroyer escorts, and support ships in the gulf are defenseless."

"Marne, Admiral Raymond Spruance with his Seventh Fleet will cover Leyte Gulf."* (260A)

The morning of 25 October, we engaged the Japanese northern fleet and annihilated it. Meanwhile, the Battle of the San Bernardino Strait ensued.* (261)

Admiral Spruance's Seventh Fleet was elsewhere.

In the next few weeks, the Third Fleet supported carrier strikes and shore bombardment on Japanese targets throughout the central and southern Pacific: Luzon, Formosa, Indochina, Swatow, Hong Kong, and Okinawa. I briefed Admiral Halsey with target folders that contained photographed and interpreted aerial images, and all-source intelligence. Using our situation map, I made recommendations about which targets to strike. My target recommendations were accompanied by details of Japanese air defenses, anti-aircraft artillery (AAA), surface and naval assets (number and type), submarine activities, and SERE operations (Survival, Evasion, Resistance, and Escape). Such combat operations continued apace until January 1945.

Fleet Admiral Nimitz ordered the *New Jersey* to our Ulithi anchorage in the Western Caroline Islands. We arrived on 13 January 1945, and Admiral Halsey transferred his flag to the newly commissioned *USS Missouri.** (262) Next day we sailed. On arrival near the Japanese Home Islands, we were a screen for our fast carriers. Beginning in mid-March, the Third Fleet hit industrial and military targets along the coast of the Inland Sea and southwestern Honshu. The Japanese responded with fierce *kamikaze* attacks,* (263) damaging several of our carriers, and damaging and sinking a host of other ships.

On 24 March, the *Missouri* joined the fast battleships of Task Force 58 in bombarding airfields and naval bases on the southeast coast of

Okinawa—a ruse to induce the Japanese high command to move military resources from the west coast to counter this action.

Battle of Okinawa, 1 APL to 21 JUN 1945

It was Easter Sunday, the first of April, 1945, and on this most holy day, the fleet Marines and Army troops stormed ashore on Okinawa's southwest coast, a prefecture of the Empire of Japan.* (264) Japanese defense strategy saw Okinawa as the last barrier to the direct invasion of the home islands. For the first time, a foreign army of 'white devils' had despoiled the sacred soil of the Rising Sun.

The Japanese were in a desperate fight to eradicate the Occidentals from their island and to keep us at bay. Our Marines and the foot soldiers, the GIs, were in a desperate fight, as the Japanese soldiers, marines, and naval infantry fought to the death. In the bloodiest conflict of the Pacific War, our casualties were extraordinary severe.

The *USS Missouri* sailed into position off the southwest coast of Okinawa. Our operation orders were to support the "grunts" in their ground operations. Our first target was the Japanese airfield at Futema.

The gunner mates in the gun houses activated the pneumatic hoist operations and a 2,500-pound general-purpose projectile from the magazine below eased into the breech of each of the nine sixteen-inch rifles. Five 110-pound powder bags of high explosives, encased in white silk, followed; last into the breech was the primer bag in black silk. The senior petty officers bolted the breach locks and notified fire control that the rifles were ready to fire. Fire control computed the mathematics needed to put the projectiles on target.

The skipper was notified that all was ready. Satisfied, he ordered, "Fire for effect."

The gunnery officer snapped the "FIRE" toggle and a vision of Hell exploded from our nine, sixteen-inch rifles' broadside.* (265)

The noise was deafening, and the recoil sent the ship slipping sideways. Folks, I gotta tell ya, that full broadside was an experience to note for all time. A dab of sympathy flashed through my mind as I envisioned the chaotic destruction and resultant inferno these nine shells would engender on the Japanese troops and even the civilians in the target area. *Vaya con Dios.*

Using all source intelligence, including directions from spotters in the air and on the ground, and of course the back channel, my team kept our target list current and prioritized. We used aerial photography for bomb-damage assessment (BDA). Two or three times a day, I briefed the Admiral and his staff on BDA and our updated target list.

And on and on it went—no respite. Throughout the days, this process continued, sending high-explosive projectiles into Japanese targets—occasionally, some twenty miles inshore. Sometimes, all nine rifles fired in broadside. Sometimes only one or two fired. The number depended on the size and structure of the target.

The Japanese reaction was aggressive, and suicidal. A strong surface force of the Imperial Japanese Navy sortied from Sasebo to counter our invasion. It was led by the super battleship *IJN Yamato** (nine, eighteen-inch rifles).* (266)

The *Missouri* screened our fast carriers as their aircraft engaged this Japanese surface squadron. I was receiving real-time intelligence and updating Admiral Halsey. We followed the action on large-scale charts in our situation spaces. Not with 100% accuracy, I might add. The action was far-ranging, fast, and fluid. From time to time, Halsey would issue a fleet order—usually it was a change of course for specific ships to counter Japanese moves, to assist damaged ships, and to assist in rescuing survivors. At battle's end, our carrier aircraft had sunk *IJN Yamato*, one cruiser, and four destroyers. The crippled remnants retired to Sasebo.

Meantime, overhead naval aircraft engaged Japanese dive-and torpedo-bombers—taking an appalling toll of their aircraft and aviators. But it was the suicide *kamikazes** (267) with high-octane gasoline and heavy-duty explosives that the Japanese used most effectively as anti-ship weapons. Thousands of antiaircraft guns from every ship in our task force spewed a gauntlet of high-velocity shrapnel in all directions. The sky was darkened with black smoke and searing metal shards. Nonetheless, far too many *kamikazes* penetrated the gauntlet and slammed into our ships with devastating explosions and fires. The resultant carnage to our ships and their crews was horrendous.* (268)

The eleventh of April was a day as all other. That is, until a Japanese *kamikaze* "Zeke" aircraft smashed into the *Missouri* close to the intelligence spaces. The explosion threw me against the starboard bulkhead. The impact broke my right wrist, and shards ripped into my left torso and left thigh. Dim light shone through the wrecked hatch. I could see that most of my men were wounded. Our spaces were in shambles, and small fires had started in some of our electrical equipment. I recall that my last conscious thought was, "Gadzooks, another Purple Heart."* (269)

Fortunately, the *Missouri* was not critically damaged. The fires were brought quickly under control, and repair parties made temporary fixes to the damage.

TWENTY-SIX

Naval Hospital, Naha, Okinawa, May 1945

I could hear the whining screams of the *kamikazes*, artillery firing, and shells exploding, occasionally a burst of machine-gun fire, and the booms of the naval rifles firing offshore. I had been in the Navy Hospital in Naha, Okinawa, for a week or thereabouts. The medicos did what had to be done: a couple of surgeries; tubes and monitors; Navy doctors, nurses, corpsmen; syringes with "square" needles filled with arcane nostrums; stitches, draining tubes, physical therapy; aides doing this and that seemingly without purpose; stethoscopes, blood pressure gadgets, and other Inquisition instruments of torture.

The primary nurse tending to me was Lieutenant Commander Yen Tou-lang, regular Navy. Her Navy aviator husband had been killed in the battle of Midway—the Operations Officer of Torpedo Squadron Eight. A delightful woman who hid her grief under a jaw-wide smile. Her tender loving care contributed mightily to my mental and physical recovery.

Damn near every morning, some caring soul entered my room, opened the blinds, and asked the irritating, "How are we doing this morning, Captain?" Egad! Enough already. Once, I actually replied with some vigor, "I feel lousy today, but I don't have a damn clue about how you are feeling." The young ensign nurse skedaddled.

That got a reaction. The senior medical officer, a Medical Corps Rear Admiral, scolded me for being insensitive to those trying to be helpful. "Aye, aye, Admiral, I'll mend my untoward ways." I was bored.

Sea duty seemed appealing compared to this hospital bed. *What's my next assignment?* The Allied invasion of the Japanese home islands was set for later this year. I had got to get involved "up to my eyeballs," as it were. Where was the *deus ex machina* to rescue me? It was irrelevant what he, she, or it would be clad in, as long as that entity had a ticket to a capital ship of the United States Navy.

I spent my healing time chatting with the Japanese medical aides to hone my language proficiency. (Those Nipponese that chose cooperation rather than suicide—which far too many of their fellows had chosen.) Most every afternoon I played chess with an Army major who had lost both legs to a Japanese mine. The fellow was a master of the game. I could not best him, but I learned. Other times, I read: biographies, history (Rome, Crusades, The Renaissance, British Empire), and the like. I was bored and needed a diversion.

Sure 'nuff. The *deus ex machina* arrived a few afternoons later. He was clad as an orderly and was pushing the book cart.

This fellow was a former Marine sergeant. But he had gotten busted to buck private for extra judicial dispatching of far too many Japanese prisoners—unceremoniously, I might add. He had gotten nicked with a bayonet by his last Japanese prisoner.

"Capt', we got some new books." He pulled one off the top shelf and handed it to me. "Try this one. It ain't no classic like the ones you've been reading. It's a thriller by Dashiell Hammett called *The Maltese Falcon*."* (270)

Characters, plot, setting, and language were captivating. Caspar Gutman's (the "fat man") famous quip, "…but we were talking then. This is actual money, genuine coin of the realm. With a dollar of this you can buy more than with ten dollars of talk." The rest was history. I was hooked on Hammett and his tales.

As I recall, it was late in the morning on the second of May, 1945. The top medico in this bedlam entered my room, maneuvered his stethoscope about my naked body in an extensive exam, and told me, "Use a cane to help you with that limp. Now, get your lazy fantail outa here and win the War."

As I was dressing, a tall fellow in a nondescript khaki uniform entered my room, eschewing the courtesy of knocking first. There were no standard identification icons on his uniform. However, on his left shoulder was a patch of some sort, and on his collars were the brass metal pins "USA."

Without ado this intruder stated, "Captain Matthew Marne, I represent General William Donovan.* (271) He wants you to join his outfit."

"Whoa there, young fella. Slow down. Where's the 'good morning, Captain'? Who the Hell are you? And where are your manners? *Comprendez vous?*"

Folks, I might have been dumb but I was not stupid. I knew that General William Donovan* was the Director of the Office of Strategic Services, the OSS* (272)—the forerunner of the Central Intelligence Agency.* (272A)

"My apologies, Captain Marne, for my imprudence. Please understand that my name is irrelevant. What's relevant is that General Donovan knows of your career and language skills, and he wants you on his team."

"That's 'more better,' young fellow. Let's have a *tête-à-tête.*"

To seal the deal, that fellow and I hoisted a few of Kentucky's finest. As I lay in my bunk in the Bachelor Officers' Quarters, with my head spinning, visions of my OSS duties popped into view: thrilling clandestine assignments where exotic, scantily-clad dames finagled the scenario to garner my secrets, by whatever means.

The next day, I was an agent in the Office of Strategic Services (OSS), a U.S. Navy Captain dressed in a nondescript uniform with those "USA" pins on my colors, and an OSS patch on the left shoulder of my shirt—an arcane signifier that only the appropriate intelligentsia could decipher.

Note the reality. My initial task was to use my marginal language skills to interrogate Japanese prisoners, the few we had. Suicide was their chosen alternative to being captured—to die for the Emperor was honorable.

I was still not whole in body. I had to use the cane and I had minimal endurance. Shortly after the end of the Okinawa campaign, sometime in late July 1945, I was working with a group of captured Japanese marines; all had been wounded but were ambulatory. Tough task. These fellows followed the Bushido Code to a fare-thee-well. Accordingly, I wasn't getting much useful information. But, once in a while, I'd harvest a nugget: Japanese intentions, force deployment, and condition and morale of the troops. The real intelligence gems were the names and locations of senior officers—some of whom were listed in our War Criminals dossier.

The interrogation routine was becoming boring. A senior petty officer could have done this job as well as I. Sea duty was especially attractive now that our fleet was operating in Japan's home waters. Nonetheless, one morning in mid-July, I was working with a Japanese marine sergeant major. This fellow wasn't going to tell "nothing to nobody," as it were. The interrogation room had no windows, and minimal air circulated through small vents in the ceiling. It was hot and humid, and my patience was fast fading.

A gunshot in the hall distracted me. As a 'dingbat' is wont to do, I glanced toward that sound. In that instant, the Japanese marine had snatched a stiletto from his boot and flicked it. In a reflex action, I twisted right, and the stiletto buried its blade in my left shoulder. You might know the location of old wounds—my left side. I drew my 1911 Colt 45 and put three rounds into that asshole's chest.

Damn, more time in my favorite hospital, and another Purple Heart.* (273) Gadzooks! As the pain suffused throughout my shoulder, my mind defaulted to wondering, how is it that this stiletto was not found during that Japanese marine's strip-down search? On reflection, the answer was easy. The U.S. Marine supervising this fellow undressing for the strip-down had not demanded, *Būtsu o nugu* (Boots off).

The pain medication had begun to dull my simple mind. I was lying on the operating-room table waiting for the anesthesiologist to complete his task and the surgeon to carve on my shoulder. For reasons I cannot explain, modified lyrics of Gene Autry's hit tune popped into my head:* (274) "Back in the hospital again, back where a nurse is a friend ...." That's all I recall. No need to detail this hospital experience. Same as all the others. 'Cept, no Maria.

It was the first of August, 1945. My left arm was in a sling, and my cane hung on a chair. I was scheduled for discharge later that afternoon. Sitting on the edge of my bed, I was supervising as an aide gathered my stuff and packed it in my duffle.

Without ado, the door slammed open and Admiral William "Bull" Halsey stormed into my room. His eyes were filled with mirth and he cracked a small smile. He approached my bed and said proudly, "Good morning, Rear Admiral Matthew Marne* (275) of the United States Navy. Congratulations, Matthew, your promotion to flag rank is well deserved." He grabbed my right hand and shook it vigorously. "How ya doin'?"

I blinked several times, eased my butt deep into my bed, and in a stumbling voice muttered, "Good morning, Admiral Halsey. Thanks for coming. Delighted to see you." I paused for a second to recoup. "Say again, admiral. I do not understand your last transmission." I was nowhere near the promotion zone. In fact, I'd been a captain for only fifteen months. I'm not an Academy graduate. In fact, I do not have a college degree. Something was afoot.

Admiral Halsey continued. "Here's the scenario. General of the Army Douglas MacArthur* (276) has demanded you by name, Rear Admiral Matthew Marne, to serve as his staff intelligence officer, and this assignment requires a flag-rank officer. And you're it. I asked most of our associates in the fleet and at Pearl, and no one had a clue how the General knew about your exploits. Irrespective, he does, and that's what counts. Accordingly, General Donovan has had orders cut for you to report to the General at his headquarters in Manila.*" (277)

He touched my right hand and said, "Good fortune, Matthew. Best get your fantail in gear. The Supreme Allied Commander, a five-star general, is waiting for you and he is more impatient than I."

With some unease, I replied, "Aye, aye, admiral."

TWENTY-SEVEN

General Douglas MacArthur's Headquarters, Manila Hotel, Manila,
June 1945

The general was a warrior of singular purpose—defeat the Imperial Japanese armed forces soonest and, from Tokyo, oversee the democratization and rebuilding of Japan into our ally.

General MacArthur dragooned the Manila Hotel* for his headquarters and residence.* (278) My primary assignment was to oversee the preparation of the 0700 hours morning intelligence report and to brief it to the General and his staff. Using all-source intelligence, I would relay the tactical situations throughout the Pacific war zones. Frequently, we would receive messages from 'Washington' sending directives, asking for information, and issuing modifications to the strategic war plan. Generally, MacArthur was dismissive of this type of communication. "Admiral Marne, take care of this crap. I don't want to be bothered with it."

"Aye, aye, sir."

However, when the establishment in D.C. tinkered with the General's tactical war plans, he got seriously interested. "Marne, do not respond to this message," was a typical response. "I know how to win this Pacific War in quick time. Most of those fellows don't know a rifle from a bazooka." He huffed and puffed, and walked away. His parting words almost always were, "Get on with it, Admiral Marne."

I did.

Deep behind the 'green door, occasionally I received information from James or Paul—my former classmates at the University of Hawaii.

Can't tell you how, even at this late date. Their information was priceless: inside information on the political discussions and decisions inside the highest echelons of the Japanese government, Spirit Warrior planning and decisions, war materials production, and morale of the populace. And, frequently their information included salacious accounts of gross misbehavior—invaluable information for post-war blackmail. What was especially telling was their information about the identification of war criminals and their crowing about the atrocities they had authorized. For example, General Prince Yasuhiko Asaka* (278A) boasted that after he conquered Nanking, his soldiers raped, tortured, and killed more than 300,000 Chinese. That hurt, seriously. Horrific images of Veronica and Mister Chong, Marine Corporal, Honorary, in the maw of the Imperial Japanese Kwangtung Army's "Rape of Nanking." My soul screamed in empathy with their agony.

In mid-July, my OSS controller sent me an 'Eyes Only' personnel message: "Contact me soonest."

General Donovan had an assignment for me. His agents working with the Viet Minh cadres* (279) in French Indochina had relayed a message from our wartime ally, the Marxist Ho Chi Minh.* (280) Comrade Ho wants a meeting with General MacArthur's representative to relay the details of his fading guerilla war against the Japanese occupiers.* (282) [And, I might add, the Vichy French Legionnaires.* (283)] His envoy would plead for the urgent need for American armed intervention in Indochina to expel the Japanese. They were sapping the life from his country. He proposed a meeting in Kunming in three weeks with the general's emissary.

General Donovan sent Ho this response, via his backdoor OSS channels: "I'm sending Rear Admiral Matthew Marne, United States Navy, as my personal representative. Admiral Marne is General MacArthur's staff intelligence officer, and an experienced 'China hand.'"

General MacArthur was not pleased. "Admiral Marne, I need you here in Manila, not chasing all over Southeast Asia. No! Tell that Irishman to stay out of my business. Get his own people to do his clandestine work."

I communicated MacArthur's response to my OSS controller.

Next morning, we had a Flash, Top Secret, Code Neptune message from the White House for General of the Army Douglas MacArthur, United States Army. "Assign Rear Admiral Matthew Marne, United States Navy, to fulfill the Office of Strategic Services request of 17 July 1945. Confirm compliance. President Harry Truman,* (281) Commander in Chief."

I reckon you can imagine MacArthur's reaction. Loyalty and prudence restrain me from saying anything more, 'cept, I plan to visit Independence, Missouri one day.

At a cooler moment, the General told me, "I am not going to invade Indochina. Tell that Communist bastard to fight the Japanese by himself. That's a backwater operation of no import." He shook my hand and said, "Get back here soonest. Later this year, I'm going to invade the home islands, and I will need your counsel. No one has the scope of your experience in this area."

Folks, I need to provide perspective for the OSS involvement with Ho Chi Minh and his Marxist cadres in Indochina. Recently, the Central Intelligence Agency gave me authorization to reveal one of the Office of Strategic Services' best-kept secrets.* (284)

For several years during the war, the OSS had been supplying Ho's cadres with weapons, communication equipment, medical supplies, and training.* (285) Some of the OSS advisors worked directly with the cadres in their guerilla campaign against the Japanese. Ho told his cadres, "The Americans have proven their friendship by giving us their wholehearted support. Treat the Americans as honored guests." His cadres rescued downed Allied airmen, and brought them to safety in unoccupied China. Several times, Ho's cadres raided Japanese prisons to rescue captured Allied airmen.

In July 1944, Ho was acutely ill and was near death. OSS medical personnel from Kunming clandestinely entered Tonkin Province and, over several weeks, our medicos administered antibiotics and other treatments to Ho. In time, he recovered and resumed leadership of his Viet Minh cadres.

(** Folks, please see my monograph titled *Ho Chi Minh and the Office of Strategic Services in World War II* for details of the OSS cooperation with the Viet Minh. It's available on Amazon Kindle.)

✳ ✳ ✳ ✳ ✳

Question: How do I get into southern China when all direct routes are Japanese-controlled: air, land, and sea?

Not easily or quickly. I traveled in mufti and the small yellow box was in my breast pocket. An attack submarine ferried me to an isolated cove on the unoccupied China coast a few miles south of Portuguese Macau. On pre-arranged signals, Red Chinese guerillas motored to the surfaced submarine and took me to shore. About a mile inland, the Chinese had cleared the land for a makeshift landing strip. Around midnight, the guerillas lit both sides of the strip with oil lanterns. Shortly, two lights low in the sky flashed brightly, illuminating the area. Almost noiselessly, an unmarked UC64 Norseman utility aircraft landed, and taxied to the east end of the strip.* (286) With the propeller ticking over, the starboard side door opened and the aviator shouted, "Admiral, get your fat ass in here *tout de suite*."

I did.

The aviator did not waste time. Before I had snapped the door closed, he had gunned the engine, and in a few seconds we were airborne and climbing steeply. He shouted, "Fasten your seat and harness belts. If I need to take evasive maneuvers, hold on." And, "You armed?" I showed him my 1911 Colt 45. Obviously, he knew my name and mission, but he did not introduce himself. The fellow was deathly quiet. Reckon he was focusing on operating this aircraft. We were en route to Kunming—600 nautical miles distant and over mostly Japanese-controlled air space.

No routine with this aviator. He frequently changed heading and altitude. Gambits to confuse Japanese air defenses. I looked carefully at the fellow, trying to assess his mettle. Wrong! That was no 'him.' The aviator clearly was female. Hard to conceal those curves even in that flying suit.

About ninety minutes into the flight, two Japanese Army Mitsubishi A5M Claude* (287) fighters attacked from our port quarter. Tracers flashed by the cockpit, and I heard *ping, ping, ping* as rounds ripped the fuselage just behind us. The aviator whipped that Norseman into a hard port turn and dove beneath the fighters' track. The Japanese aircraft circled and started their next attack. On cue, the *deus ex machina* appeared as a white, puffy, cumulus cloud. We disappeared inside. The remainder of the flight was without Japanese interceptors—thanks to whomever.

It was early morning when we landed at a small strip about ten miles from Kunming's city center. I extended my hand to the aviator and said, "Thanks. Much appreciate your skills."

She snapped, "Forget it." She went around the Norseman inspecting the bullet holes, accessing the damage. Expletives abounded. Non-ladylike, I might add. Apparently, the damage was mostly cosmetic, nothing to keep the aircraft grounded.

An OSS officer greeted me. He was in uniform, and wore a Smith and Wesson 357 Magnum in a shoulder holster.* (288) "Welcome to China, Admiral Marne. My name is Jim [*nom de guerre*], and I am your contact, chauffeur, and major domo. You've met Jane, her *nom de guerre,* the pilot of the Norseman. I've booked a suite for you at the Blue Parrot Hotel. It's about four miles from the city center—far enough away for us to conduct business." I piled into an unmarked American jeep with my small duffle, Jim kicked the jeep in gear, and we left in a cloud of dust.

The hotel was ensconced in beautiful, flowering, shade trees, and surrounded by carefully tended gardens. It was old, I reckon from the last of the Qing Dynasty. Yet it was well tended and had modern amenities— probably from a major renovation in the mid-1920s. I would classify the Blue Parrot as a boutique hotel for the affluent and those who wanted their trysts to be confidential, and for OSS business.

I walked to the desk to register. Jim took my arm and vectored me to the elevator. "Admiral, we've made all the arrangements." Inside the suite, he handed me the key and said, "Sign for everything, we'll cover all your expenses. Let me know what you need."

"I need a change of khakis, fresh underclothes, toiletries, a shot of Kentucky's finest, and sleep."

"You'll have it shortly." He lit a cigarette, fussed about a bit, then went to the writing table and used a fountain pen to write in black ink on a slip of hotel stationery. "Careful what you say in this room. The Juntang,* (289)

Dai Lis,* (290) Chinese Bureau of Investigation and Statistics, have bugged these rooms. Burn all written communications."

Not surprised, I responded, "I understand. Will do."

We walked to the suite's veranda and continued our conversation.

Jim continued. "This hotel is nearly fully booked. A number of our people, Chinese officers, several businessmen, and a few *filles de joie,* who work directly for the Juntang."

"I hear you."

"Last word we've had from Ho's staff is that his agent is en route. They did not tell us who. Nonetheless, his agent is late, should have been here yesterday."

"Trouble?"

"Maybe. But I think not. Ho's cadres would ensure a clear route from Tonkin."

"I'll stand by." Jim left and I slept for several hours. I awoke at twilight. My closet had several new khaki uniforms, and there were fresh toiletries and a safety razor on the dresser. I headed for the bar, and ordered a double shot of Kentucky's finest. With libation in hand, I ambled to a small tea house in the garden. The twilight was lovely and the aroma of blossomed flowers set a scene far from the interminable war being waged across the Pacific. For the first time in years I began to relax—relax deeply, and my mind wandered through images I should have forgotten. *I'm so tired of the killings. Will it end next year? The year after? Or, yet one more year?* I sipped the bourbon and wondered, *Of shoes, and ships, and sealing wax. Of cabbages, and kings. And why the sea is boiling hot with shot and shell and mangled bodies. Gadzooks! Marne. What jabberwocky has gripped your soul?** (291) In my reverie, I had failed to notice an Oriental woman standing at the entrance.

"May I join you? It is so lovely outdoors this evening."

I rose and replied, "Please do, madam."

"Thank you. You are so kind."

I withdrew a chair for her. She moved gracefully. "May I order for you?"

"Indeed. Green tea with a dab of brandy."

Her English was excellent. She was of indeterminate age. In the coming darkness, I could not see her eyes. She had a pronounced limp and used a cane. Her black hair was tied in a bun and had touches of grey. She wore a dark grey sham fu that fell to her flat-heeled shoes. And she appeared to be somewhat overweight. Perhaps fifty years old. Hard to tell.

A barmaid brought her spiked tea. My visitor sipped the potion delicately. She formed a slow smile and said, "That is nice. Thank you, Admiral Marne."

Whoops! Already something is afoot. I stood and stared at the woman. "Madam?"

She retained her smile and responded, "Let us enjoy the fading twilight and our delightful beverages." What minimal conversation we had was desultory and of no import. Nonetheless, my mind raced. Who? Why? And my 1911 Colt 45 was in my room.

Soon we were engulfed in darkness on a moonless evening. She rose, and broke the silence. "Admiral Marne, let us go to your suite to continue. The mosquitos are sucking my life's blood."

With hardness in my voice, I replied, "Madam, you have me at a serious disadvantage." Without reflection, I blurted, "Who are you? Friend or foe?" Whoops. That was a dumb outburst.

She rose, and touched my left shoulder gently. "Friend. I have a message from an old acquaintance."

My simple mind whirled with confusion, questions, and caution. Into what rabbit hole was this *femme fatale* leading me? Soon, I reckoned, *What the Hell, let's explore this dame's game plan.* "Madam, Chinese intelligence has my suite bugged. We should walk in the garden to chat."

"You fellows in Western intelligence are far too simplistic. My associates have introduced static in all their transmitters throughout the hotel, and have clandestinely sabotaged their receiving and recording equipment in the basement—without fingerprints. The damage was ascribed to a natural occurrence due to a power surge." She took my hand and we began to stroll. "We will be safely away from the chicanery of Generalissimo Chang's fascist intelligence service."

I stopped. "Madam, please, I do not mean to be rude, but before we continue I must know who you are and what your scheme is, your protocol, and how it involves me." Anger rose in my voice. "And who is this old acquaintance?"

We stopped. "Very well, Admiral Marne. For now. My Christian name is Bethel—truly it is. And I bring a message for you from Minister Chou En-lai."

The dim light in the back of my mind shone. I understood.

I flicked the light switch on in my suite. I grabbed the telephone and ordered a bottle of Kentucky's finest, a bottle of brandy, and a porcelain pitcher of green tea.

"Admiral, your order is prescient. I am seriously thirsty." She tossed her cane on the floor, threw her arms upward, and twirled about several times. Her skirt flared and I caught a glimpse of a well-turned ankle that was not shocking. Rather, the leg that showed was delightful. (*Mea culpa*, Cole Porter.)* (292) Say again, over. What's happening? That Red *femme d'une certaine âge* was out of character.

With a sense of urgency, Bethel announced, "I am suffocating in this stupid masquerade." She sat on the bed, kicked off her shoes, and threw a small rock at me. "My limp, Admiral." She stripped the band off her bun and long, black hair cascaded over her shoulders. She used her fingers to comb her hair and the grey disappeared. She stood and ripped off the sham fu, and twirled about twice. She looked boldly at me with large almond eyes that sparkled, and with a provocative smile asked, "How am I doing, Admiral Matthew Marne of the United States Navy?" She twirled again. "I'm no madam. I am a *mademoiselle* and damn proud of it."

Over my career in the Orient, I have seen and cared for (may I say 'loved'?) some gorgeous women. But, I must tell you that Bethel was near the top. She was a startlingly beautiful and sensuous woman. She wore a red, skintight cheongsam, slit to the upper thigh. A golden dragon embroidered on her cheongsam wrapped its way sinuously around her bewitching body. She had a wide, full-lipped mouth; high cheekbones; glowing, pale-olive skin. Her legs were long and shapely, and her wasp-thin waist enhanced her near-perfect figure.* (293)

I stared at her for several seconds. Her exotic beauty and coquettish mien had me flummoxed. Not what I expected or was prepared for. Flashing through my simple mind was, Why would Minister Chou choose such a *femme exotique* as his envoy? *Quién sabe.* Reckon I'll know shortly.

Proudly, she announced, "If Chairman Mao could see me now, he would have me sent to a re-education camp for anti-revolution activities." She paused. Stood with her arms akimbo and legs spread. That slit was at her waist. "Perhaps he would have me shot for corrupting the peoples' morals." After a slight, thoughtful pause she blurted, "And who is that bastard Mao to enforce morality? He is a libertine of first order. He has seduced or raped most every young woman in our encampment."

The soft knock on the door said that my beverage order had arrived. I asked Bethel to go into the bathroom and be silent. The waitress placed the beverages on the center table and left.

Bethel returned, more subdued, as the adrenalin subsided. "Please pour a brandy for me. Make it a serious double, with a spot of green tea."

I did. And a double whisky for me.

She took the snifter, performed the traditional procedures, and sipped the libation with a touch of grace. "Thanks, Admiral. That brandy is charmingly delightful. We had no such libations with the Red cadres. Potable water was a luxury."

Bethel sat on the chaise lounge. And I in the chair at the writing table. I did notice that the slit in her cheongsam inched up ever so slightly from to time.

"Bethel, why are you wearing this provocative cheongsam? It is lovely. And it does suit you extremely well. It is so out of character for your background and important mission."

She stood, extended her arms, and slowly turned around again, displaying her sensuous body for my appreciation. "I want to be free. I want to be a woman, and to enjoy all the things women do: adventures, seductions, and engaging in the activities that I choose—not what some Red apparatchik decrees. Not a cog in a collective. I want to do what pleases me, not what's in those commissars' diktats. I am not going to kowtow to their commands. I am finished with those fascist Communist dullards."

Made sense, but irrelevant. "Bethel, I hear you. I empathize with your goals, and I'm hoping that you realize your dreams. Now, we need to focus on your mission."

She snapped out of her reverie, returned to the chaise lounge, sipped her brandy at length, \and said nothing as she reorganized her thoughts. "Please excuse me, Admiral Marne, for diverting us from the serious business at hand."

"Very well." I looked straight into her beautiful eyes. "Bethel, for you to be trusted with a secret message from Minister Chou, I must assume that you work for Kāng Shēng's* (294) Ministry of State Security,* (295) True?"

She dropped her head slightly as she formulated her response. "Admiral, you are correct. I am an agent of the Ministry and I report directly to Director Shēng." In a semi-apoplectic voice she said, "I am a ministry agent because it is the easiest way to survive Communist tyranny."

"Bethel, my mission to Kunming is Top Secret. I must know how Minister Shēng knew of it."

She fidgeted in the chaise lounge. "I am reluctant to reveal Minister Shēng's intelligence secrets. Such an impudence is fraught with danger."

"I understand. However, it is critically important that I know of this break in our communication system."

Bethel stared at me for a few seconds as she evaluated her options. She took the brandy bottle and poured more than a double portion of the liquid into her snifter. Without comment, she took a "healthy" swig. And another.

Sensing that she needed a touch more insinuation to reveal the key, I demanded, "Bethel, if we are to continue our parlay, tell me how Minister Shēng knew of my mission."

Resigned, she slumped in the chaise lounge, crossed her ankles, and folded her arms across her chest. Finally, she began, "You are signing my death warrant if you reveal the secret I am going to reveal."

"Bethel, you have my word as a flag officer of the United States Navy that I will classify your information at an extremely high level. Only those very few in my community that have a verified need to know will see it, and only one of those will take appropriate action."

Now in a more relaxed voice, she said, "It's simple. Ho Chi-Minh's senior radio operator is an agent for Minister Shēng. In off hours, she sends him messages encrypted in a Chinese code. On the surface, Mao's Red Chinese and Ho's Viet Minh cadres are friendly allies. Not true. Longtime hostilities pervade this so-called alliance." She reached for the snifter and swigged deeply. She used a cocktail napkin to wipe her lips. "That's beautiful. Heavenly, if I may say."

"Indeed, it is. Please continue."

"Alright. Chairman Mao and his cadre are miffed, and I might say jealous, that Ho Chi Minh and his Viet Minh are allied with the United States in their fight against the Japanese, and the Vichy French. Ho's cadres receive tons of military and medical supplies. They know that your doctors saved Ho's life. And they know about Ho's and General Giap's* (296) entreaties to Presidents Roosevelt and Truman for a formal alliance or incorporation as a commonwealth of the United States of America."

Whoops! I did not expect those nuggets of HUMINT (human intelligence). Nonetheless, critical for our wartime ally in Indochina.

"Thanks, Bethel. Be assured that your secrets are secure." I finished the glass of Kentucky's finest, and prepared another. Such critical information needed slow and critical evaluation. And, I was in a puzzlement. *Why had not our 'Q' people intercepted these Viet Minh off-the-record messages and decoded them?* First priority was to understand and fix that on my return to Manila.

It was time to turn to the business at hand. "Very well, Bethel, what is Minister Chou's message?"

"Minister Chou invites you to visit him in Yunnan Province to observe his Eighth Route Army's campaign against the Japanese Kwantung Army. Our weapons are old and there are no replacements except those captured from the Japanese. The troops are chronically short of ammunition, and the wounded lie dying without medical aid and narcotics to ease their crossing. And Stalin's Soviets are slow, very slow to support us. The belief among the Party's apparatchiks is that Stalin wants the Japanese and the Chinese Communists to expend themselves in conflict so that the Soviets can occupy Manchukuo and China's northern provinces without a fight."

"So I understand." I swigged Kentucky's finest. "In summary, Chou needs American weapons, and medicines, and wants me to be the facilitator. Correct?"

"In essence, yes. Admiral Marne, I am to escort you to Yunnan Province."

Whoops! Impossible. There was no way I could honor Chou's invitation. I could not allow the Red Chinese to have control of my movements. It would be the red pill in the yellow box without doubt. "Bethel, I cannot travel to Yunnan. I do not have permission, and I would not go even if I had permission. The United States supreme command in Washington would not authorize it, and General of the Army and Supreme Allied Commander Douglas MacArthur has instructed me to return to Manila as soon as possible. That's his order."

She nodded in acceptance. "Minister Chou anticipated that you would decline his invitation. In such a case, he has instructed me to ask you to plead his request with the senior authorities in your country: light arms, heavy weapons, ammunition, and medical supplies including those miracle drugs that fight infection effectively."

Kentucky's finest warmed my soul and sharpened my rational mind. I may be dumb, but I'm not stupid. Chairman Mao would vector his Eighth Route Army with USA arms full force on Generalissimo Chang Kai-shek's National Government the hour the Japanese were defeated. In a few years, Mao's Red army would conqueror all China and turn it into a Stalinist state. Following that, the detentions, mass killings, disruption of civility and customs, and resultant chaos would be horrific. I further ventured that Mao's reckoning and transformation would be many times more severe than what the Japanese had inflicted on occupied China. I was not going to facilitate the Communist victory over Chang's nationalist government—our ally, of a sort.

"Give my warm regards to Minister Chou. I remember well our association in 1939 and the sacrifice his troops made to facilitate my escape. Tell him that I sincerely regret that I may not visit him. Nonetheless, I will send with dispatch, and under my signature, his request to key Washington authorities—those few who have the authority to approve, or not, Chou's request." *I'll do it alright. And the exalted grand poohbahs in Washington will file it in the trashcan, posthaste.*

"I am wishing that good fortune will follow him in his endeavors. That he may remain safe and in good health. I will summarize his Eighth Route Army's gallant fight against the Japanese Kwangtung Army and integrate it with his requests."

"Admiral Marne…," she gasped. Threw her hands to her face and began sobbing uncontrollably. After a time, she regained enough composure to murmur, "I do not want to return to Communist-controlled Yunnan. Tonight, I am free! I am free of those tyrannical Communist bastards." And with a loud and firm voice, "I am not returning." She took her snifter and emptied her brandy without ceremony.

What now? This woman had me perplexed. Two shots of Kentucky's finest later, a faint light flickered in the deepest recesses of my simple mind. And like an Indianapolis 500 racer, it sped to the forefront. "Bethel, you sound firmly committed to foregoing your return to Yunnan Province. Please consider my question and respond forthrightly." I looked directly into her eyes and in a strong voice asked, "Is your resolve unequivocal?"

"Admiral, I am determined. I am Chinese and will remain in the Nationalist-controlled areas of China. That's final."

"Perhaps, Bethel. Perhaps. Please consider, however, that there are serious obstacles that would hinder fulfillment of your goal to remain in unoccupied China."

She cocked her head, and looked at me with that *What the Hell are you talking about?* stare.

"You are an agent of Minister Shēng's Communist intelligence organization. The Nationalist Juntang would quiz you intensely with a myriad of relevant, and irrelevant, questions. If your answers are not satisfactory, and they seldom are, your pain would be excruciating. The questioning would continue unrelentingly for days. Eventually, your interrogators will have eviscerated your soul. You will either be dead, or so broken in body and mind that you would no longer be human."

Bethel's eyes widened. She threw her hand to her mouth, and uttered a small scream. She stared at me as my words penetrated her being. She refilled the snifter, drank the brandy, and returned the nearly empty glass to the side table. Eventually, she asked in *sotto voce*, "Is that the truth, Admiral Marne? Your narrative is horrifying. I am loathe to believe it." She almost emptied the snifter. "I could not endure such torture."

"Bethel, if you have a respected sponsor, one that would vouch for you and take you under their protection, such Juntang unpleasantness might well be avoided."

She relaxed deep in the lounge chair as the reality of a possible way out of her predicament became apparent. She delayed her response as she considered my point. "What kind of a sponsor?"

"The American Office of Strategic Services—our intelligence agency."

She blinked several times as the outrageousness of my suggestion suffused through her mind. Interested, she asked tentatively, "What would your intelligence agency require of me?"

"Stand by." I called Jim. "Come to my suite. I may have an opportunity for you to exploit."

No need to discuss the preliminaries. Jim got to the point. "Bethel, the OSS would be your sponsor if you would undertake a long-term assignment for us inside Mao's senior cadres."

"I do not want to return to Yunnan." She considered her options. Somewhat confused, she asked, "What assignment?"

"Before we can trust you with details, we must confirm that you are truthful and sincere. Are you willing to take a polygraph examination?"

"Maybe. I've heard of these truth machines. Does it hurt?"

"Not at all. However, we must search you thoroughly beforehand. We have a female agent in the hotel."

Bethel looked at me, asking for advice or approval.

I nodded my head sideways several times and held my hands palms up.

She closed her eyes and slid back in the chaise lounge. Eventually, she said, "I accept."

She and Jim left. I knew the drill. Jane would strip Bethel, and search her hair and elsewhere.

Jim returned. "Jane is conducting the test. So far, so good. Bethel may be our first opportunity to insert a double agent into Mao's senior political elites. Lots of details to construct, but it is workable. If she is clean, I have the authority to make a deal with her."

"What about her people that sabotaged the 'bugs' in the hotel?"

"Bethel confirms that they are at another location, and awaiting her signal to return to Yunnan. She has not said how she will signal them."

An hour or so later, Jim left to get Bethel. When the pair entered, Jim was smiling ear to ear, and she was clad in a dull grey housecoat.

Jim announced gleefully, "She passed. Twice."

Bethel was nervously concerned. "Admiral, I am troubled. My previous agent assignments were simple things—easily accomplished and minimally precarious. But this double agent assignment is dangerous. If betrayed, I will suffer a long and painful death. Tell me your thoughts, please."

"*Mademoiselle* Bethel, I am at a loss to advise you. Jim is your contact."

Sensing Bethel's hesitancy, Jim interrupted, "Bethel, here is our deal. You will send us information about the inner workings of Chairman Mao's Communist Party and his Eighth Route Army: plans, personnel and operations, anything you deem important. If we know, or even suspect, that you've been compromised, we will extract you posthaste."

"Waiting for you will be $250,000 in United States dollars in the Manufacturers and Traders Trust Company in New York City,* (297) a new identity with papers to prove it, and a permanent visa or citizenship in the Western country of your choice."

She stood. Looked at Jim and me as if we had additional incentives. Getting no response, she commented, "Your incentives are enticing. Alright. I'll do it." She stood and approached Jim. "Is it not appropriate in Western cultures to shake hands to conclude the deal?"

"Indeed, you are correct."

As Jim and Bethel shook hands, she looked at me. "Admiral Marne, you are my witness."

"Indeed, I am, *mademoiselle*."

The pair returned to Jane's room to discuss communication procedures and all manner of "spook" stuff. Stuff I do not, and do not want to know.

I sipped my whiskey and wondered, *What have I wrought?*

Sometime later, Bethel returned, finished her brandy and stated, "I'm tired and going to retire." She walked towards my bedroom, slipped out of her housecoat, and vanished inside.

It happened that I was tired also.

❋ ❋ ❋ ❋ ❋

Bethel was gone when I awoke. Her cheongsam was hanging in the closet, and her disguise clothing was gone. I reckoned that this unforeseen episode was *la fin*.

I milled smartly about the hotel for a couple of days waiting for the Viet Minh envoy. Reading, enjoying the gardens, and appreciating the delicious fare of the restaurant. Jim did not speak of Bethel—no longer my concern.

Jane returned late one afternoon, and proudly announced that her Norseman looked and flew like a real airplane again. "All the Japanese holes are patched. Thank you."

It was late the next afternoon, the third day of waiting. I was in my suite reading Ernest Hemingway's* (298) *A Farewell to Arms,* (299) and wearing my OSS outfit. The rap on the door was slight and barely discernable. The fellow was Oriental, of medium height, somewhat thin, in need of a shave, and clad in a dark brown, western suit that had seen better days.

He looked exhausted. Nonetheless, I recognized him immediately.

"Am I addressing Rear Admiral Matthew Marne of the United States Navy?" he asked softly.

"Indeed, you are correct. Please come in, General Võ Nguyên Giáp." I noticed that his right sleeve was covered in blood and that there were splotches of blood on his vest and shirt.

General Giap shuffled into my suite. "May I sit?" Without response, he plopped on the chaise lounge. "Please excuse me. The last few days have been difficult."

"I see, general. Stand by." I called Jim. "Our guest is here. I need you and Jane here soonest. Bring clothing and have Jane bring her medical kit—enough for in-room surgery."

"I do not want to cause you trouble. I will rest for a few minutes."

"Nonsense, General Giap. Now you are in the care of the Office of Strategic Services. Let's get you out of those clothes." He stood and held onto the arm of the chaise lounge. I undressed him. His body was blood-stained. The wound in his arm was severe and oozing blood. A gash on his chest was about four inches long and festering.

The pair entered. Jane, with keen professionalism, assessed the general's medical condition. "Shave the general's hair. All of it. Everywhere. Wash him thoroughly in the shower with this antiseptic solution."

Jim and I did. We stripped my bed, tucked a clean sheet over it, and laid Giap on it. Jane injected a double dose of morphine in the large vein in the bend of his left arm, and the general went to 'la, la' land. That female OSS agent did what she had to do with surgical skills. She extracted a Japanese bullet from his arm, cut and cleaned his chest laceration, dusted sulfonamide on both wounds, stitched them closed, applied bandages, and jabbed his butt with a large dose of penicillin. "The general ought to be okay in a few days. Give him one of these penicillin pills every four hours. And change the bandage twice a day. Understand?"

"Yes, mam," I responded.

"I'm leaving in my Norseman on an assignment. Ought to return in four or five days. Let the general have my room." And she vanished.

Jim answered my unasked question. "Jane has had extensive training in field-medicine at our off-the-books camp in southern Virginia."

To summarize: Jim and I nursed General Giap for several days. He regained most of his strength and mobility, and he wore the OSS khakis—without identification.

His story was simple. "The Japanese ambushed my squad. I am the only survivor. Must have had intelligence on our route. I've no idea how they knew. Perhaps a turncoat in our camp seduced by the reward, or careless use of our radios. We will find out."

I opted not to tell General Giap Bethel's secret. He's a smart *hombre*. He'll find the turncoat soon enough.

❈ ❈ ❈ ❈ ❈

Folks, I'm going to interrupt this narrative to set the background for this meeting with General Giap in Kunming.

President Roosevelt, at the Atlantic Charter Conference in August 1941, stated that he demanded the end of colonialism, and he affirmed the right of all peoples to choose their form of government.

At the Tehran Conference in late 1943, President Roosevelt demanded that the French end their colonial rule in Africa and Indochina, and insisted that "the people of Vietnam are entitled to self-government."

In one telegram to the president, Ho proposed making Vietnam an overseas protectorate of the United States—something akin to the relationship with the Commonwealth of Puerto Rico, or an unincorporated territory, as is the Virgin Islands or Samoa. Ho was willing to trade Vietnamese independence for American patronage, in lieu of French imperialism or Chinese suzerainty. He even offered to adopt the American Constitution.

❈ ❈ ❈ ❈ ❈

Let's return to Kunming.

General Giap asked for the coat from his suit.

"General, your suit of clothes was not salvageable. We burned it in the hotel's incinerator a couple of days ago."

"For the best. Perhaps you found a small pouch in the breast pocket."

"Yes. It is on the side table." Also on the table were Giap's Viet Minh identification papers, French passport, and various currencies. I handed the pouch to the general.

"Here is a small token we have prepared for President Roosevelt for his generous support of our cadres' fight for independence, and his promise to free us from the French colonial oppression." He handed me a small gold emblem engraved in Vietnamese script. He said, "It is inscribed 'Thank you, President Roosevelt.'" He looked about and spotted the water pitcher on a side table. "May I?"

"Permit me, General." I poured the water and handed it to him.

"*Merci.*"

"We are saddened to acknowledge that President Roosevelt has died. Since he was our sole patron, I ask you to see that the American people know of our love for him and your great country."

"Be assured, General Giap, that I will make certain that the citizens of the United States know of your heartfelt gift to our late president and country."

"Admiral Marne, the Pacific War is moving toward its conclusion. Chairman Ho and I had sent messages to President Roosevelt asking him to keep the French colonists out of our country, and to work for a postwar political and economic integration with the United States of America. Unfortunately, he did not respond, and we are at a loss to know why. Now, we are distressed that President Roosevelt has died. Two months ago, I sent a telegram to President Harry Truman asking him to open a dialogue with us to discuss details of President Roosevelt's commitment to Vietnam and for some sort of a legal affiliation with the United States. This is our sincere desire. Again there has been no response."

"I am at a disadvantage, General Giap. I have no knowledge of such promises and requests. I know of the OSS material support for your cadres, but I do not have details. And, I must tell you that I am not privy to your communication to my presidents. Nor do I have insight into their decisions."

"Perhaps you can discover if President Harry Truman will fulfill President Roosevelt's promise to the Vietnamese." He sipped deeply. "Without a response, we are perplexed. And fear greatly that the French colonialists will return. If not the French, certainly it will be the Chinese."

He paused to form his key point. "Admiral Marne, I am here in Kunming to ask you, a respected warrior from the Yangtze River Patrol and other honorable activities in the Orient, to present our proposal to President Truman and plead with him to consider with objective reality the major strategic advantage a political and economic union with Vietnam would bring to the United States and to all Southeast Asia. Soon, the Chinese Communists will overrun all China, and they will covet the natural treasures of my country and all those nearby."

Whoops! General Giap's requests were far outside my ken. How could I respond without mucking up our wartime relationship and maybe beyond? My immediate reaction was to sympathize with the Vietnamese proposal. However, this was top-level White House and State Department business.

"General Giap, I am grateful that you have such regard for me to ask that I present your proposals with conviction to our commander in chief. Simply, I do not have the military or political standing to be the paladin for the Vietnamese with the politicians in the White House."

"Chairman Ho and I understand your position. We ask that you do all in your power to get our messages into the process, and follow through, and ask that you maintain communications with us through the OSS agents in Kunming and Tonkin."

"General Giap, you have my word."

"*Merci beaucoup*, Rear Admiral Matthew Marne. I had prepared copies of our messages to the White House. Unfortunately, my portfolio was lost in the fight with the Japanese." He paused. "I shall make copies and send them to you via our OSS contacts. Will that be satisfactory, Admiral?"

"Indeed, your proposal is satisfactory. I will include it in my report to Headquarters Naval Intelligence and with my hearty endorsement."

"*Très bon*. Then, I shall leave."

"With respect, general, you are recovering from two serious wounds. And I do not know of any arrangements you have to return. You must remain here until our aviator and her Norseman aircraft return. She will fly you to Chairman Ho's sanctuary." With absolute authority, I concluded, "No protestation."

Defeated with logic, he said, "We have a small strip. Our cadres keep it disguised. On my signal, they will make it ready."

Folks, that's all for this chapter. Some of you may wonder how President Truman responded to the Vietnamese requests. Answer: Dien Bien Phu, May 1954; Tet Offensive, January 1968; and the fall of Saigon and evacuation of the American Embassy, 30 April 1975.

My return to Manila was roundabout and slow. Jane flew me to Chunking. I rode 'the Hump' (the Himalayas) in a Curtiss C46 Commando.* (300) Landed at Assam, India; PBY Catalina to the Andaman Islands, to Perth, Australia; Darwin; Lae, New Guinea; Davao City, Mindanao, Philippines; to Manila.

TWENTY-EIGHT

General Douglas MacArthur's Headquarters, Manila Hotel, Manila, Early July 1945

Intensive planning for the invasion of the Empire of Japan's home islands consumed us on General Douglas MacArthur's staff. Operation Downfall was set for 1 November 1945. Elements of three army divisions would land on Kyushu and Honshu islands. Using all-source intelligence, we knew that Japanese resistance would be fierce in defense of the sacred soil of the Chrysanthemum Throne against the Occidental white devils.

Sleep, when I could afford it, was at my desk. Hot, black coffee and grilled cheese sandwiches were my sustenance. Target planning was the overriding priority for my team. And, I resumed my responsibility for preparing and delivering General MacArthur's morning brief. The demanding routine melded night into day into weeks of no discernable difference.

It was about the first of August. Around midnight, a "Q" messenger handed me an Eyes Only, Top Secret message from General Donovan. He had forwarded this communication from Chou En-lai. "For Rear Admiral Matthew Marne, United States Navy, Manila. I am regretful to tell you that Chang Ying (Bethel) has had a serious accident and cannot fulfill her contract with your OSS."

So, that was it. *C'est la guerre.*

*****

At 0815 hours on 6 August, the B29 aircraft dubbed Enola Gay* (301) dropped the nuclear weapon "Little Boy" on Hiroshima.* (302) The resultant blast and firestorm caused wide-ranging devastation to the city and extensive civilian casualties. The Spirit Warriors in Tokyo* (303) refused President Roosevelt's demand for unconditional surrender and vowed to follow the Bushido code to fight to the death.

On 9 August, the B29 named Bock's Car* (304) dropped an atomic bomb on industrial Nagasaki. Again, the devastation and casualties were horrific. Now convinced of the futility of continuing the war, the political elite in Tokyo urged the God Emperor Michinomiaya Hirohito* (305) to announce the cessation of hostilities and to seek peace.

At long last, this horror in the Pacific was over.

USS Missouri, Tokyo Bay, 25 September 1945

The *USS Missouri** (306) was anchored in Tokyo Bay—Admiral William Halsey's flagship. A hundred ships of the Third Fleet crowded the bay. A thousand American flags and red, white, and blue bunting fluttered in the morning breeze. Overhead, a host of naval aircraft flew in the "V" formation.* (307)

General of the Army Douglas MacArthur,* (308) Supreme Commander of Allied Forces, Pacific, stood on the *Missouri's* quarterdeck. His arms were akimbo, and his eyes were focused on the accommodation ladder. I stood just a few feet behind and to the left of the general. Standing to my right was General Jonathan Wainwright,* (309) the hero of Corregidor.

The Japanese delegation from the Empire of Japan came aboard,* (310) + (310A) without honors rendered. General MacArthur spoke eloquently, and signed the documents.* (310B) The Japanese officials affixed their personal Kanji glyphs to the instrument of surrender.* (311) At long last, this ghastly odyssey was ended. Flashing before me were images of the aircraft of the Imperial Japanese navy attacking the *USS Panay* and of my dead and wounded shipmates. Reckon all were spouting large grins.

✻ ✻ ✻ ✻ ✻

My assignment as an OSS agent was "Special Staff Intelligence Officer" on General Douglas MacArthur's staff. My duties included finding Japanese war criminals, interrogation of key civilian and military personnel, and most anything the General could conjure. We operated out of the Da-ichi Life Insurance Building* (312) in the Yurikucho District in Tokyo. The devastation from the B29 iron-and-fire bombing raids was dreadful. Vast areas of the city were wasteland and rubble.* (313) I wondered how the Japanese people could have endured this long.

There is a God! One beautiful autumn afternoon in late October, the *deus ex machina* stood at my desk. He was escorted by two armed military policemen. He was dressed in the uniform of a Japan Air Transport pilot.* (314) He bowed deeply and said, "Good afternoon, sir. I have come voluntarily to offer information on a war criminal." He had a pronounced limp and relied on a cane.

Another one? Every day, I interviewed three or four of these fellows, usually ex-Japanese military, willing to offer a tip on the location of a war criminal. Universally, their goal was to have their dossier expunged, earn a reward, and ingratiate themselves into our good graces to get an Occupation job. Most of these tips were fictitious; however, from time to time we'd make an arrest.

Most of the Spirit Warriors, and the top rogues on the wanted list, were either under arrest or had committed *hari-kari*. For instance, we had captured General Hideki Tojo at his home just seconds before he was to commit suicide.

The fellow stood patiently waiting for my response. "Why do you wear the uniform of a Japan Air Transport pilot?"

"I was seriously wounded in the war and discharged as unfit for duty. Our civilian airline company, JAT, was desperate for aviators. They hired me as a copilot for the Nakajima L2D aircraft.* (315) Even today, I am an employee of JAT."

For reasons I cannot explain, this fellow presented a mien that piqued my interest. "Very well. Who are you?"

"Thank you." He bowed again. "I am former navy aviation officer

Lieutenant Masatake Okumiya. My war record is honorable."

"We will decide that. Continue to the point."

He stood stiffly at attention and spoke in a clear and authoritative voice. "I know the location of Prince Yasuhiko Asaka* (316) of the Imperial House of Japan, and the uncle of Emperor Hirohito."

Whoops! This fellow purported to know the location of the Japanese officer who ordered the attack on the *Panay* and sanctioned the Rape of Nanking:* (316A) Prince Asaka, the number-two war criminal on our wanted list. Good fortune or another hoax? Let's see about this ex-naval officer.

"How do you know this information, Lieutenant Okumiya?"

"Please, sir, with your permission, I would sit in this chair?"

His body motion betrayed that he was having difficulty standing. "Indeed, do so."

Seated and in a strong voice, he continued, "At one time before the Chinese War, I was an aide to Prince Asaka. On a day in early March 1937, we rode in his staff car for about 70 kilometers west of Tokyo to the village of Alami, in the Shizuoka Prefecture. He had a small house on a rocky out-cropping overlooking the bay. As my duties were universal, I arranged for the food, the sake,* (317) and the geishas* (318) with their samisens."* (319)

He paused to gather his thoughts. So far, his presentation had the ring of authenticity. Perhaps it was because I wanted to believe him. Prince Asaka was one asshole I desperately wanted to bring to justice.

Lieutenant Okumiya continued. "Early the next morning, the sake bottles were empty, the geishas were dressed and gone, and the Prince was drunk on the pleasures of the evening. He asked me in a stumbling voice why I had not joined him in the evening's festivities. 'Sir, it is my duty to have my wits at all time to best serve you.'"

"The Prince smiled in approval and began to speak with bravado, 'If the Empire of Japan is to become a great nation we must have the natural resources of East Asia. The only way we can control the rubber, oil, and iron, and all the other resources we need is to take them from the Occidental colonialists by waging war. The Supreme War Council has concluded that we must provoke the United States and the European colonial powers into a war. Our strategy is to be aggressive in East Asia, and to cause mischief to vex the Americans. Our opening gambit was to invade Manchuria in 1931 and make it our puppet state. In four months, the Imperial Army will provoke an incident in China and our troops will conqueror Peiping and the large coastal city. Our goal is not to conquer China—impossible—but to provoke the Occidentals into a supreme conflict that we will win easily in 1937. I am thirsty. More sake, you!'"

"I always have a reserve—a small bottle in my valise. I filled his glass, and he drank it swiftly. I poured another. Satiated, he continued, this time in a doleful voice."

"'The Occidentals are weak, engulfed in the Great Depression, and the United States endorses isolationism. Our army will wade ashore in Long Beach, California, in just a few months.'"

"I was shocked at the Prince's secret information and deeply concerned about the aftermath of such a strategy. 'Sir, I understand,' I said."

"Prince Asaka continued with stumbling words. 'The Spirit Warriors in Tokyo are in error. The Americans are not stupid. President Roosevelt will not respond with military power, rather he will make some diplomatic protest and increase the sanctions on oil imports. Realizing that war with the Empire of Japan is inevitable, the United States will began a vigorous arming program, and they will overwhelm us in the eventual war. No doubt.' He swigged the last drop of sake. 'The white devils will despoil the sacred soil of our homeland. I will be labeled a war criminal and hunted. But I will elude them. I will hide in this *minka* under an assumed name, and become a fisherman."

"Admiral, that is my true story."

I wonder. Could be. "You have told an interesting story. How am I to believe you?"

"I am an honorable man. A naval officer from a proper family."

"Do you know that there is a reward of two hundred thousand United States dollars for information leading to the arrest of Prince Yasuhiko Asaka?"

"Yes, sir."

An interesting fellow who projected cachet. "Tell me about yourself."

"I was an aviator of a Yokosuka B4Y Type 96 dive bomber during the China campaign. In December '37, I was the section leader on a mission to attack a large convoy of Chinese boats in the Yangtze near Hoshien. Hostile fire hit my right hip and leg. On recovery, the medical board determined that I was unfit for duty, and I was discharged. Since then, I am a pilot for Japan Air Transport."

Whoops! Could it be? "Tell me, Lieutenant Okumiya, what else do you recall about that attack on the Chinese boats?"

"It was on a Sunday afternoon sometime in mid-December."

Beginning to sound like it probably could be. "Maybe your war record is not so honorable. We'll have to investigate."

"I assure you that I had nothing to do with the Rape of Nanking. I was in the hospital at Chefoo." He looked at the senior military policeman.

"Sir, we searched his folio carefully. Nothing of interest."

Okumiya opened his folio, withdrew a batch of papers, and handed them to me. "You will see that I am honorable."

His documents confirmed his story, absolutely.

I returned his documents. "Tell me more about your attack on those Chinese boats, Lieutenant." My mind was on full alert.

He sensed that I was trying to entrap him. He dropped his head and his eyes stared at the floor.

"Did you see any markings or flags on those Chinese boats—the Occidental gunboats, Lieutenant?"

In a contrite voice, he said, "Sir, you know my secret shame. Yes. The American and British flags were prominent. " He squirmed in the chair and tried to look me in the eyes, but could not. "I beg to offer my apologies for my unprovoked attack on the *United States Ship Panay* and His Majesty's Ship *Ladybird*, the death of the American and British sailors."

"When you saw the flags of neutral countries on the gunboats, why did you not abort your mission?"

"Impossible. Prince Yasuhiko Asaka ordered the attack on the neutral ships—a chapter in his mischief. To disobey would mean beheading and dishonor to my family."

And there it was. The truth at last from a naval aviator who had led the attack on the *USS Panay*. Perhaps it was I who had shot him. *¿Quién sabe?*

"Lieutenant, you give an interesting account of the attack on the *Panay* and *Ladybird*. We need to confirm it. Would you agree to submit to a polygraph examination?"

"Of course. I must make contrition, I now am a Christian."

"Very well. On completion of the examination, we will take you into custody, for your protection, until we arrest Prince Yasuhiko Asaka."

He started to protest, then slumped back in the chair and said, "Yes. Of course, I understand."

I stopped my secret Dictaphone recorder, and addressed the two military policemen. "When we have Lieutenant Masatake Okumiya's comments transcribed, I'll need your signatures as witnesses to the authenticity of the document."

"Yes, sir."

❊ ❊ ❊ ❊ ❊

The Japanese police had Prince Asaka's house surrounded and were out of sight. I wore my dress blue uniform with medals. (I had a slight port list.) I carried my 1911 Colt 45 in my left hand. I nodded to the senior plainclothes detective at my side. With his gun drawn, he kicked the front door askew and rushed in, followed by three other policemen. We found the Prince watching television, a John Wayne war film, "The Fighting Seabees."* (320)

Resigned, he offered no resistance. "I knew you would come one day."

I approached the fellow. "Prince Yasuhiko Asaka, I arrest you in the name of the International Military Tribunal for war crimes: the illegal attack on the *USS Panay* and *HMS Ladybird*, the torture and massacre of Chinese civilians in Nanking, and other war crimes documented in your dossier." He was nonplused, and stared at me with dull eyes. The police handcuffed him and led him to one of their automobiles. At last, the bastard would face justice.

Gadzooks! The Prince did not experience justice. After several weeks in custody, he was released and not charged. Reckon it had to do with politics. He was a prince of the royal family and General MacArthur was working to engender empathy and a working relationship with these Japanese royals to forge them into democratic allies of the United States.

I signed the papers to release Lieutenant Masatake Okumiya and ordered the military police to bring him to me. "Lieutenant Okumiya, here is your cashier's check for 7,600,000 yen ($200,000 US). I would caution you to change your name, move to the southern island, and start a different profession. Eventually, the Prince will realize it was you who betrayed him, and he will seek revenge. The Yakuza* (321) will be looking for Lieutenant Masatake Okumiya."

"Aye, aye, admiral."

TWENTY-NINE

General Douglas MacArthur's Headquarters, Tokyo, July 1947

For two years I had been busting my fantail tracking Communist activities in Japan; doing interrogations and special green-door assignments; writing intelligence reports on Mao Tse-Tung's Communist insurgency in China; providing details on Soviet clandestine intelligence activities in Manchuria and Korea; and more.

I was exhausted in body and soul. The war had been long and painful and my work demanding to a fare-thee-well. I needed time away from the hubbub, time to relax, to read, to walk unconcerned, with my 1911 Colt 45 in my locker. I took my leave slip directly to the general.

"Admiral Marne, you're the best man on my staff. I need you here in Tokyo to help me get the rot out of Japan, get it functioning as a Western-style democracy, and frame it into our ally. Those damn Commies across the Sea of Japan are going to cause big trouble soon." He drew on his corn-cob pipe. "Here's the deal, Rear Admiral Marne. No leave. I'm going to issue you a set of orders that will allow you travel anywhere in the Far East and the Pacific Environs to which you have been verbally instructed. Your assignment is to gather information about the 'state of the area.' Class 1A, Air Priority, and unlimited expenses." General MacArthur shook my hand and with a slight smile said, "Shove off, Yangtze sailor."

My first stop was Nanking. The portfolio of Chinese stamps remained in the naval intelligence vault. Nanking was in shambles. Eventually I found the area where the cobbler shop ought to be. It was not there. In fact, the alley was not there. The entire area was a pile of rubble. Images of the Japanese horrors inflicted on Veronica and her father, Mister Chong, infused my soul. I tried to shake the scenes away. Didn't happen. At the Embassy's basement bar, two double shots of Kentucky's finest chased the demons away for a while. How long had it been? Seven years, it was. My passion for Veronica had faded some time ago. Nonetheless, I was obligated to see her, perhaps to rekindle the old flame, and surely to return the stamps to her father.

I stayed at the remains of the American Embassy for a week, trying to find Veronica and Mister Chong or any trace of them. To no avail. I made official and local inquiries. Nothing. The answers were strikingly similar:

"The Japs destroyed everybody and everything of the inferior race."

"You are on a fool's errand."

"All the people from this area were tortured to death."

"I do not wish to recall the horrors I saw."

At least three-hundred thousand, likely many more, Chinese civilians were slaughtered in the Rape of Nanking—acts of horrifying barbarity carried out on the orders of Prince Yasuhiko Asaka. It was painfully obvious that that my search was futile.

Resigned, I flew to Hong Kong on a Royal Air Force C47 Dakota* (322) and checked into the Repulse Bay Hotel.* (323) I booked a large suite overlooking the bay. Two servings of Kentucky's finest did not ease my mental pain. My mind whirled with virtual images: U-boats, Marfa, Eugenia. Radio school, *Panay*, Navy Cross, back channel, attaché, Veronica, Chinese stamps, Admiral Nimitz, *USS Missouri*, *kamikazes*, hospital, pain, Purple Heart, General MacArthur, service alone, and thousands more. Two double Bourbons later, I climbed into the bed and slept. I awoke later in the evening and was wolfishly hungry. I called room service and ordered a porterhouse steak, well done (Texan preference) with all the trimmings.

Next morning, I made the decision. I'd had it. Time to retire and to go home. I had had no leave for more than five years. My parents had died while I was in the Central Pacific, and I missed their funerals.

The naval attaché at the diplomatic mission sent several messages for me:

To the Bureau of Personnel, requesting immediate retirement.

To General of the Army Douglas MacArthur, Supreme Commander of the Allied Forces: "I'm not returning to Japan, I am retiring from the naval service and the Office of Strategic Services. I am going home to Texas. Thanks, Grand Poohbah of the Universe. Best of fortune."

To Major General William Donovan, OSS: "I quit. Retiring soonest."

It was over! Finally, it was truly over. I was done. *Acabado*! For the first time in years, I cracked a large smile. At the hotel bar I celebrated my liberation with several bottles of Mum's finest, sharing them with the other patrons. I was at the bar chatting with a British army major, when a charming *femme d'une certaine âge* approached and said, "Your champagne was most welcome and delicious. Permit me to order another bottle."

"Please do." The lady spoke with English broad vowels and her mien exuded a touch of Empire. The major, a perceptive fellow, skedaddled to other climes. The innkeeper popped the cork and poured.

She toasted to good fellowship all 'round. And I followed. Surprisingly, she did not introduce herself or ask my name. Our badinage was light and of no import. At a lull in our chitchat, she stated, "My husband is the *chargé d' affaires* in this Hong Kong British Crown Colony and he is on temporary assignment in Kuala Lumpur."

Folks, I may be dumb but I'm not stupid. I do not philander with married women. Period.

Her subtext was all too obvious. I glanced at my wristwatch and said, "Madam, thank you for the champagne and your excellent company." I rose and shook her hand. "I must say goodnight. I have an early morning flight tomorrow. Best of fortune."

Next day, I booked a flight on Pan American World Airway's China Clipper to Oakland. There is a God. First class on Pan American is an experience "to experience." Infinitely better than a narrow canvas seat on cold, drafty, military transport aircraft.

En route, the radio officer handed me a message. It was from General Douglas MacArthur. "Rear Admiral Matthew Marne, United States Navy. Fair winds and following seas."

An hour later, the radio officer handed me another message. This one from General "Wild Bill" Donovan. "No one quits the service. Your name is on our honor roll of Distinguished Service Members. Within the next few months, the Office of Strategic Services will evolve into the Central Intelligence Agency. Please visit us."

These messages engendered peace in my soul. Truly, I had concluded my back-channel career. One might wonder how these fellows knew I was on that flight. I suspect it was 'the fine Italian hand' of the Hong Kong Naval attaché.

A few days later I was in Marfa and a civilian. I sent the Chinese stamps to the Smithsonian Institution's National Postal Museum, and stowed my 1911 Colt 45 in a footlocker.

That's all folks. *Adios*. See y'all next time.

FIN

Nota bene:

My dad, Rear Admiral Matthew Marne, United States Navy, retired in July 1947 after thirty years' service. A few months later, he married my mother, the widow Eugenia Maria (nee Barrister) Mackeson. Admiral Marne adopted me, and I took his name. He gave me his 1911 Colt 45. My parents lived on the Pinto Canyon Ranch and kept the ranch functioning.

Ever see a Rear Admiral, riding a galloping quarter horse, lasso a careening steer? A real cowboy, as it were.

Rear Admiral Matthew Marne, United States Navy (Retired), *USS Panay* survivor, died peacefully in his sleep on 11 August 1976. He was buried in Arlington National Cemetery with full military honors. That Marine in his dress blues handed me the meticulously folded American flag.

Captain, Matthew Marne, Jr., USN
Naval Air Station North Island, Coronado, California
25 December 2000

ADDENDUM 1
Photographic Gallery

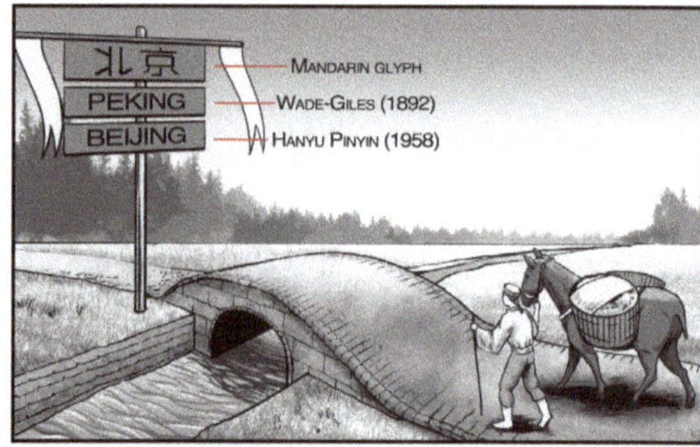

2. Wade-Giles Spelling

3. *USS Panay*

4. Battleship Row, Pearl Harbor, 7 December 1941

5. The Punch Bowl, Honolulu

6. Radioman Badge, Chief
Petty Officer

7. Imperial Japanese Kwangtung Army Enters
Nanking, 13 December 1937

8. Engine Order
Telegraph

9. Japanese Kwangtung Army Instigates "The
Rape of Nanking," Mid-December 1937

10. United States of America 48-Star Flag

11. Admiral
Harry E. Yarnell, USN

12. Rear Admiral Mitsunami Teizo,
Imperial Japanese Navy, IJN

13. General Tang
Shengyshi, Chinese
Republican Army

14. *HMS Ladybird*

15. *HMS Bee*

16. Standard Oil,
Socony Vacuum

17. Mei Ping

18. Chinese Junk

19. U S Naval Hospital Subic Bay

20. Purple Heart
1st Award

21. Silver Star

22. Bronze Star
with Combat V

23. Navy Cross

24. Purple Heart, 2nd
Award with
One Cluster

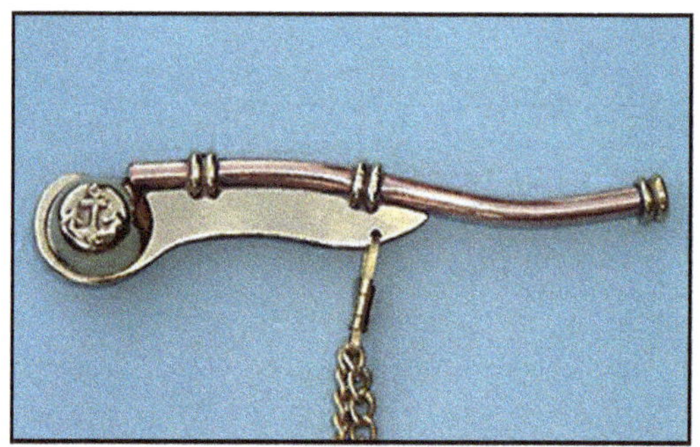

25. Boatswain's pipe

26. Navy
Expedition Medal

27. China
Service Medal

28. Sul Ross State University, Alpine, Texas,
Circa 1920s

29. The Great War, 1914

30. Great Britian Flag

31. Republic of France Flag

33. German Empire Flag

35. President
Woodrow Wilson

34. German Submarine WWI

36. *SS Housatonic*

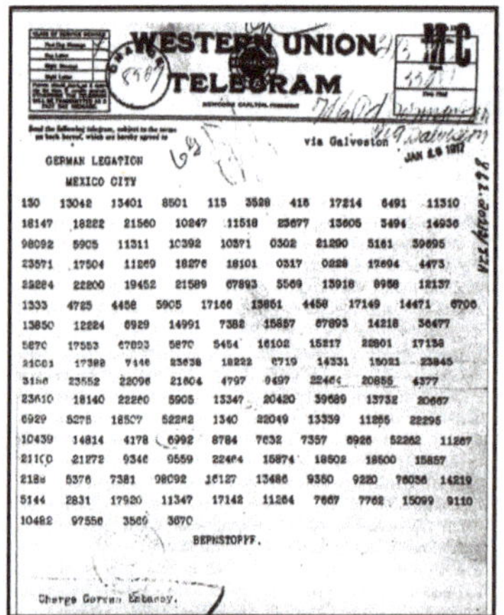

37. The Zimmerman Telegram

38. British MI6 Emblem

39. Republic of Mexico Flag

40. Texas State Flag

41. U.S.A. Declares War on Imperial Germany,
6 April 1917

42. U.S. Navy Recruiting
Poster, Circa 1917

43. Radioman Striker
Chevrons on Dress
Blue Uniform

44. *USS Porter* DD59

45. Radioman Third
Class Chevron on
Dress Blue Uniform

46. German Unterseeboot, WWI

47. German Zeppelin

48. Bronze Star

49. Texas Tech University, Lubbock, Texas,
Circa 1920s

50. Davis Mountains, Texas

51. Rio Grande River in the Big Bend Area

52. Kodak
Brownie Camera

53. Ford Model T Roadster, 1923

54. 1920s Flappers

55. Pinto Canyon Ranch, Chinati
Mountains, Texas

56. Pinto Canyon Road, Chinati
Mountains, Texas

57. Herford, White Face Cattle

58. Branding Cattle

59. String Barbed Wire

60. Bronco Busting

61. Davis Mountains, Texas

62. The Ghost Town Pueblo Nueva,
Big Bend Area, Texas

63. Mountain Lion

64. Diamondback Rattlesnake

65. Smith and Wesson 38, Model 1905

66. 1911 Colt 45

67. Radioman Second
Class Chevrons on
Dress Blue Uniform

68. The Agricultural and Mechanical College of
Texas, College Station, Texas, Circa 1930s

69. Radioman First
Class Chevrons on
Dress Blue Uniform

70. Saltwater Crocodile

71. Wallabie

72. Inland Taipan Reptile, Australia

73. The Southern Pacific's "Sunset Limited," 1920s

74. Chrysler Four-Door Model 72, 1928

75. Barnum & Bailey
Circus Poster

76. Dorothea Lange
Symbolic Photograph,
The Great Depression,
1930s

77. Captain Haynes
Ellis, USN

78. Chief Petty Officer
Radioman Badge on
Dress Blue Uniform

79. Chief Petty Officer Combination Hat

80. Navy Gold Service Stripes

81. Chief Petty Officer
Dress Blue Uniform

82. Enlisted Service
Dress Blues

83. Japanese Glyphs

84. Pan Ameican China Clipper

85. *USS Arizona*, BB39

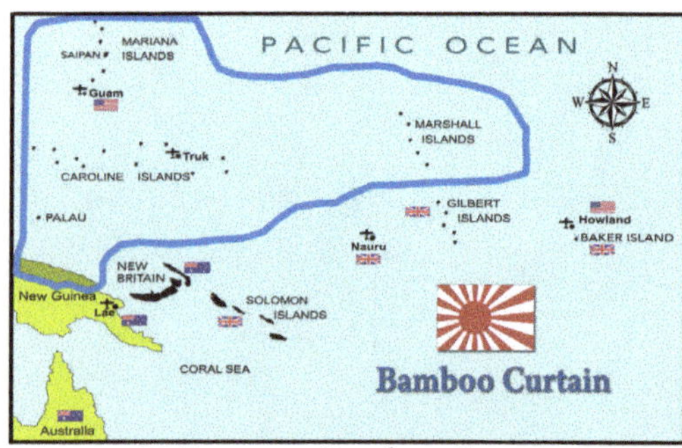

86. Japanese Bamboo Curtain

87. Captain Lewis
"Chesty" Puller, USMC

88. Augusto
Cesar Sandino

89. Purple Heart,
First Award

90. President
Franklin Roosevelt

91. Bronze Star with
Combat "V"

92. Pan Am World Airways China Clipper

93. Street Scene Singapore

94. Soda Plant at Trona, CA

95. National University of Singapore

96. British Foreign
Intelligence Service,
MI6, Emblem

97. Raffles Hotel, Singapore

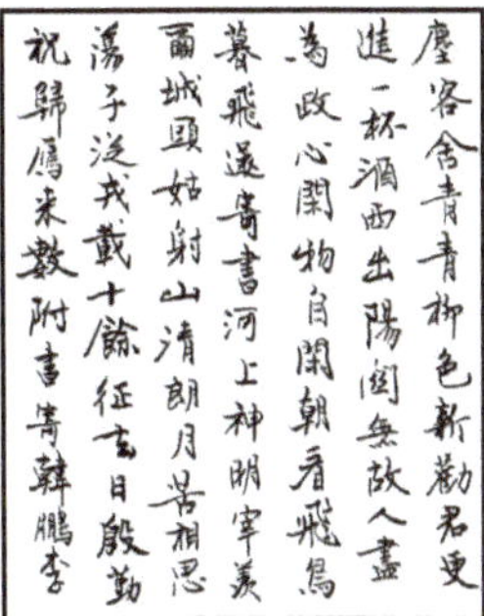

98. Mandarin Glyphs

99. Chinese Newspaper

99a. Republic of China Flag

100. State of Manchukuo Flag

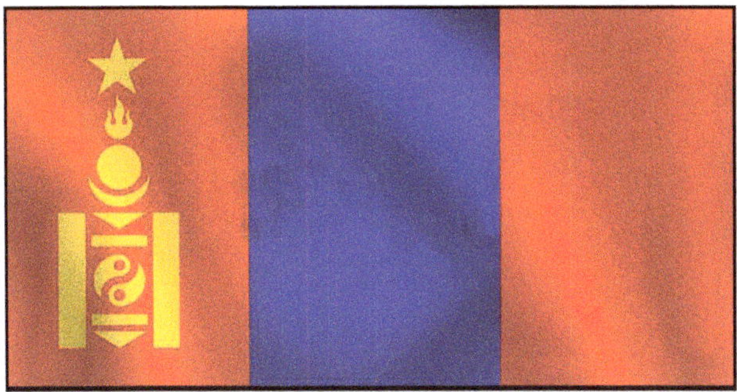

101. People's Republic of Mongolia Flag

102. Sinkliang Province, China

103. Warlord General
Marshal Chang Tso-lin

104. Generalissimo
Chang Kai-shek

105. Bowie Knife

106. Chinese Cobra

107. *USS Panay*

108. The Bund, International Settlement, Shanghai, 1928

109. U.S. State Department Research & Intelligence Emblem

110. Hong Kong Street Scene

111. *HMS Ladybird*

112. Warlord General
Lu Jung-t'ing

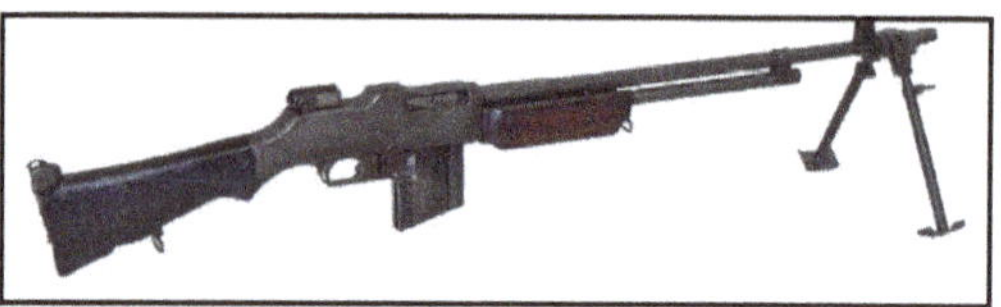

113. Browning Automatic Rifle

114. Thompson Ssubmachine Gun

115. Oretsky's White Russian Tea House

116. Marco Polo Bridge, Peking, Circa 1930s

117. Chinese Boxers,
1901

118. Tartar Wall, Peking, Circa 1900

119. Colonel Sir Claude
MacDonald, GCMG,
GCVO, KCB, PC

120. U.S. Marines on the Tartar Wall,
Peking, 1901

121. Chinese Cannon, Circa 1900

122. Captain John T. Myers, USMC

123. Empress Dowager Tz'u-hsi

124. U.S. Marine Campaign Hat with Emblem

125. 1897 China Imperial Post, Small 4¢ on 3¢ Red Revenue Stamp

126. His Wu Lake Park, Nanking

126A. Naval Aircraft Factory PN Amphibian

127. Imperial Japanese Kwangtung Army
Enters Nanking

128. Imperial Japanese Kwangtung Army
"Rape of Nanking," Mid-December 1937

129. Reserve Colonel
Kingoro Hahimoto,
Imperial Japanese
Army, IJA

130. General Prince
Asaka Yasihiko, IJA

131. Nakajima A4N, Type 95

132. Yokosuka B4Y1 Type 96

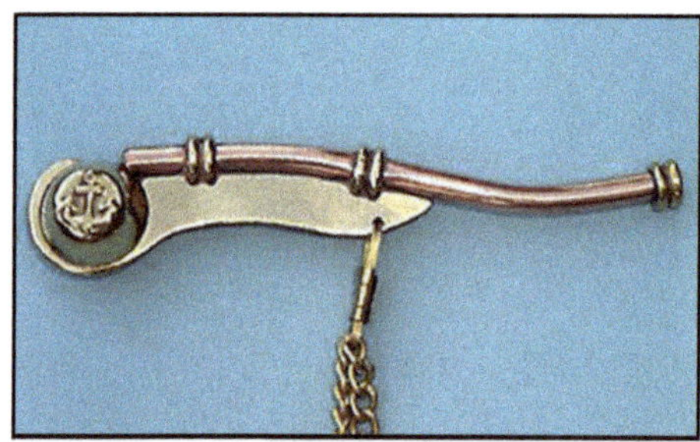

133. Boatswain's pipe

134. Brodie Helmet, 1917

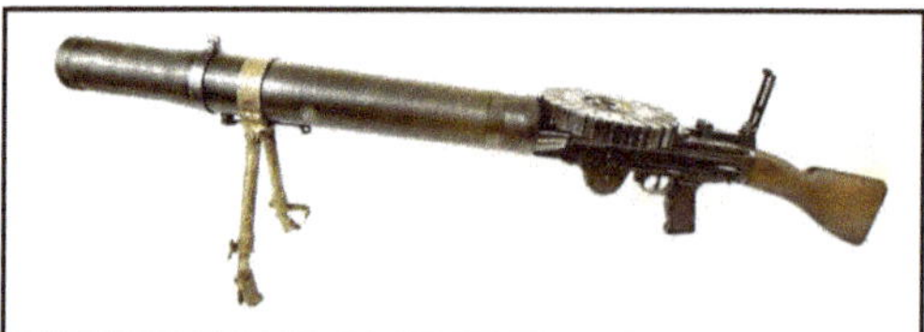

135. Lewis 30-caliber Machine-gun

136. Ambasador Joseph
C. Grew

137. Japan Foreign
Minister Hidrto Koki

137A. President Franklin D. Roosevelt

138. Rear Admiral
Mitsuami Teizo, IJN

138A. Cordell Hull,
U.S. Secretary of State

139. Captain Morihiko
Miki, IJN

140. Sulfanilamide

140A. Consolidated PBY Catalina

141. Rear Admiral
Ralston S. Holmes,
USN

142. Lieutenant
Stripes on Dress
Blue Uniform

143. Naval Air Station Pensacola

144. Navy Lt in Dress
Whites Uniform

145. Navy School of Photography,
Pensacola, Florida

146. American Embassy Tokyo, 1941

147. Leica II

148. Black Dragon
Society Emblem

149. Kiyomizu Temple, Kyoto

150. Imperial Japanese Kenpeitai Soldiers

152. U.S. Navy Summer
Mess Dress

151. Marine Musician

153. Rear Admiral, Walter S. Anderson, USN

155. Empire of Japan Flag

154. Lieutenant Commander Sleeve Stripes on Dress Blue Uniform

156. Union of Soviet Socialist Republics Flag

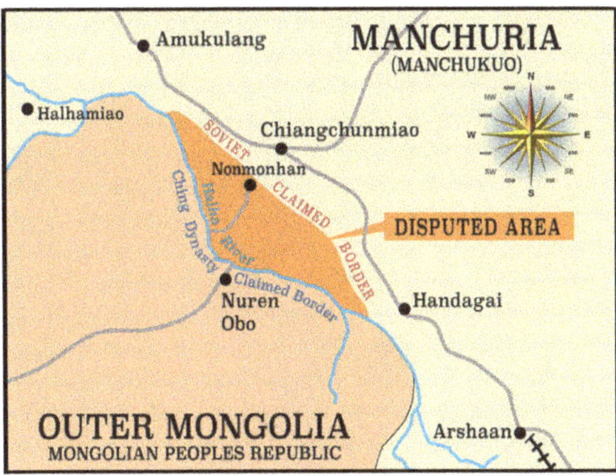

157. Nonmonhan Map Disputed Area

158. Train on China Eastern Railroad (CERR),
Circa 1930s

159. Russian Fleet at Tsushima Strait

160. Field Marshal
Hajime Sugiyama, IJA

161. Mitsubishi G4M1

162. Leica IIIa

163. Brown Belt First Kyu Symbol

164. Female
with Shamisen

165. Nakajima Ki 27 with Nmonhan
Campaign Chevrons

166. Kenpeitai
Emblelm

167. Mongolian Yurt

168. Joseph Stalin, General Secretary of the Communist Party, Union of Soviet Socialist Republics, Circa 1930s

169. Marshall Georgy Zhukov

170. Lubanka Prison, Moscow

171. Soviet Artillery in the Nomonhan Conflict, 1939

171A. "Hopalong Cassidy Returns" Motion Picture Poster

172. William C. "WC"
Fields, Cinema
Actor/Comedian

173. The People's Com-
missariat for Internal
Affairs (NKVD)

174. Packard 12 Automobile, 1939

175. German *Wehrmacht* Advances in Poland,
September 1939

176. Chancellor Adolf
Hitler of the
Deutsches Reich

176a. Adolph Hitler

177. Lavrentiy Beria
Head NKVD

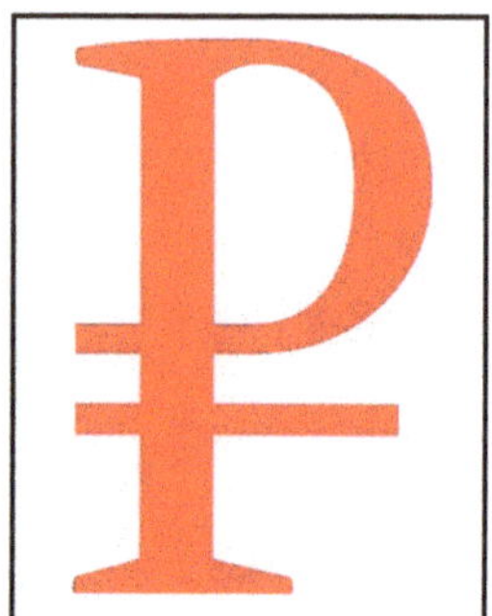

178. Symbol for the
Soviet Ruble

179. $50 Gold Certificate

180. Soviet Union
Internal Passport

181. Admiral James O.
Richardson, USN

182. Republic of China,
Kuomintang Emblem

183. Comrade Mao
Tse-tung, Chairman of
the Communist Party
of the People's Republic
of China (PRC),
Circa 1930s

184. Rear Admiral
Walter S. Anderson,
USN

185. Comrade Chou
En-Lai, Minister of
the National Security
Council, PRC

186. Kodachrome 1940s Pkg

186A. Mitsubishi A6M Zero

187. Japanese MTB

188. *USS S-16*

189. Dining Room, Peninsula
Hotel, Hong Kong, Circa 1938

190. Rickshaws, Tokyo, Circa 1940

191 Eastman Kodak Company Logo

192. US Embassy Tokyo, 1930s

193. Imperial Japanese Naval Aircraft Attacks U.S. Fleet,
Pearl Harbor, 7 December 1941

194. Battleship Row Pearl Harbor Attack

195. The Punch Bowl, Honolulu

196. United States of America Declares War on
Empire of Japan, 8 December 1941

196A. Minister
Shigenori Togo,
Foreign Affairs Office,
Empire of Japan

197. Imperial Hotel, Tokyo, Circa 1941

198. Frank Lloyd
Wright, Architect

199. Old Imperial Bar, Imperial Hotel, Tokyo, 1942

202. *USS Langley CV1*

200. Japanese Pacific Conquest

201. *USS Houston CA30*

203. *HMS Prince of Wales*

204. *HMS Repulse*

206. *HMAS Arunta*

205. Swedish *MS Gripsholm*

207A. Polana Seerena Hotel

207. Manning the Rails

208. George VI, King of the
United Kingdom and the
Dominions, 1940s

209. German U Boat WWI

210. Royal Air Force Short Sunderland Seaplane

211. Browning 303 Machine Guns

212. *MS Serpa Pinto*

213. Rear Admiral
Theodore Wilkinson,
USN

214. Admiral Earnest
King, USN

215. Bronze Star with
Combat V and One Pip

216. Fleet Admiral
Chester W. Nimitz,
USN

217. Bataan Death March, March 1942

218. Commander
Joseph (Jo) Rocheford,
USN

219. Symbolic Image of
Women Accepted for
Volunteer Emergency
Service (WAVES)

220. University of
Texas Tower

220A. University of Southern California

221. Lord
Alfred Tennyson

222. Lieutenant
Colonel James Dooittle,
United States Army
Air Corps Reserve
(USAACR)

223. Granville Brothers Gee Bee Model R
Super Sportster

224. General of the Army
George C. Marshall, USA

225. B25 Mitchell Launches from the
USS Hornet CV8, 18 April 1942

226. *USS Hornet CV8*

227. General, Prime
Minister Hideki
Tojo, IJA

229. Imperial Japanese Navy

228. Marshall Admiral
Isoroku Yamamoto, IJN

230. *USS Enterprise CV6*

231. *USS Yorktown CV5*

232. Guadalcanal Solomon Islands

233. Major General
Alexander Vandergrift,
USMC

234. Martin PBM Marnier

235. Commander
Sleeve Stripes on Dress
Blue Uniform

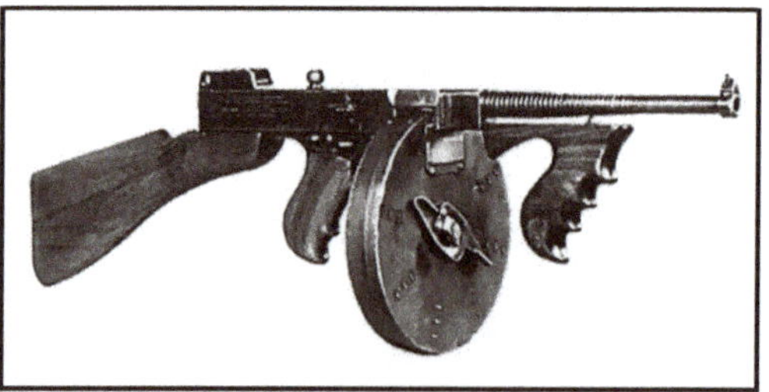

236. Thompson 45-Caliber Submachine Gun
with Type C Drum Magazine

237. Grumman F3F Wildcat

238. Vought F4U Corsair

239. Lockheed P38 Lightning

240. Consolated BPY Catalina

241. Brewster F2A Buffalo, Royal Netherlands
Air Force

241A. Royal Dutch Air
Arm Emblem

242. Purple Heart with
Two Clusters

243. *USS Solice AH5*

244. James Robert
(Bob) Wills, American
Western Swin
Musician, Circa 1943

245. Silver Star

246. *AHS Centaur*

247. Lobby, St. Anthony Hotel, San Antonio, Texas

248. The Alamo Mission, San Antonio

249. The Colonial Room Bar, Menger Hotel, San Antonio

250. San Jose Catholic Mission, San Antonio

251.The Rose Window
in the San Jose
Catholic Mission

251A. Anacacho Ballroom, St. Anthony Hotel,
San Antonio

252. Rear Admiral
Rosco E Schuirmann,
USN

253. Admiral William
F. Halsey, USN

254. *USS New Jersey BB62*

255. Captain Stripes

256. Fleet Anchorage Near Ulithi Atoll,
Caroline Islands, Circa 1944

257. General of the
Army Douglas
MacArthur, USA

258. Leyte Island,
Commonwealth of
the Philippines

259. General of the Army Douglas MacArthur
Wades Ashore at Leyte

260. Vice Admiral
Jisaburo Ozawa, IJN

260A. Admiral
Raymond A Spruance,
USN

261. Battle of San Bernardino Strait, 23–26
October 1944

262. *USS Missouri BB63*

263. Japanese Kamikaze Pilot, Circa 1945

264. American Marines, Okinawa Campaign, April 1945

265. *USS Missouri BB62*, Nine-Rifle Salvo

266. *IJN Yamoto*

267. Japanese Kamikaze Attacks, Okinawa Campaign, April 1945

268. *USS Franklin CV13*

269. Purple Heart with
Three Clusters

270. The Maltese
Falcon novel

271. Lieutenant
General William J.
Donovan, USA

272. Office of Strategic
Services (OSS) Emblem

272A. Central
Intelligence Agency
(CIA) Emblem

273. Purple Heart with
Four Clusters

274. Orvon Grover
"Gene" Autry, "The
Singing Cowboy"

275. Rear Admirasl
Sleeve Stripes

276. General of the
Army Douglas
MacArthur, USA

277. Manila Hotel, Circa 1939

278. Living Room, General MacArthur's
Apartment, Manila Hotel, Circa 1945

278A. General Prince
Asaka Yasihiko, IJA

279. Viet Minh Flag

280. Ho Chi-Minh

281. President Harry S. Truman

282. Imperial Japanese Flag

283. French State Flag (*Régime de Vichy*)

284. CIA Emblem

285. Office of Strategic Services (OSS) and Ho Chi Minh

286. Noorduyn UC-64A Norseman

287. Mitsubishi A5M, Claude

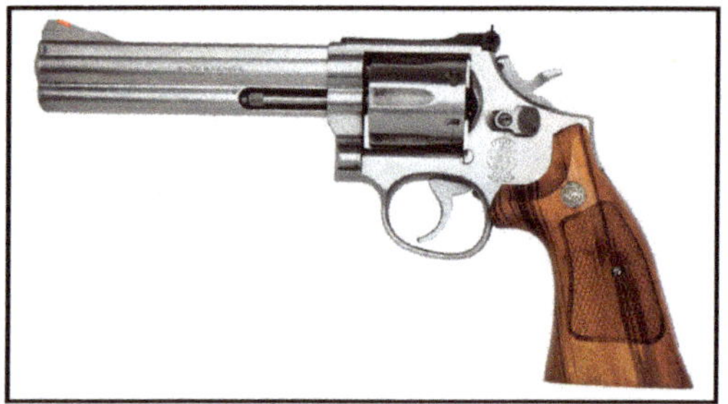

288. Smith and Wesson 357 Magnum

289. Symbol of the Juntang Bureau of Republic of China's Kuomintang

290. Minister Dai Li, Head of the Juntang Bureau, 1944

291. Charles Lutwidge Dodgson, Pen Name "Lewis Carroll," Circa 1850

292. Cole A. Porter, American Composer and Lyricist, Circa 1943

293. Bethel

294. Comrade Kang Sheng, Minister, Office for the Elimination of Counterrevolutionaries, PRC

295. People's Republic of China, Ministry of State Security Emblem, Circa 1945

296. General Vo
Nguyen Giap

297. Manufacturers
Trust Bank NYC

298. Ernest M.
Hemingway, American
Journalist, Novelist,
and Sportsman, 1945

299. Movie Poster, "A
Farewell to Arms," 1932

300. Curtiss C46 Commando Over the
Himalaya Mountains, "The Hump"

301. Boeing B29 Aircraft Dubbed "Enola Gay"

302. Atomic Weapon "Little Boy" on Hiroshima

303. General, Prime
Minister Hideki
Tojo, IJA

304. Boeing B29 Aircraft dubbed "Bockscar"

305. Japanese Emperor
Michinomiya Hirohito,
Circa 1940s

306. *USS Missouri BB62*

307. U.S. Navy Aircraft in Victory Flyover, Tokyo Bay, 2 September 1945

308. General of the Army Douglas MacArthur, USA

309. General Jonathan M. Wainwright IV, USA

310. Japanese Delegation on *USS Missouri*, 2 September 1945

310A. Japanese Delegation on board
USS Missouri

310B. General MacArthur signs
formal surrender

311. Japanese Officer Signs
Cease Fire Document

312. Dia Ichi Building Tokyo

313. Tokyo in Ruins, Circa August 1945

314. Japan Air Transport Pilot in Uniform

315. Nakajima L2D

316. General, Prince Asaka Yasihiko, IJA

316A. Japanese Kwangtung Army "Rape of Nanking," Mid-December 1937

317. Traditional Sake Service

318. Geisha

319. Geisha Playing Shamisen

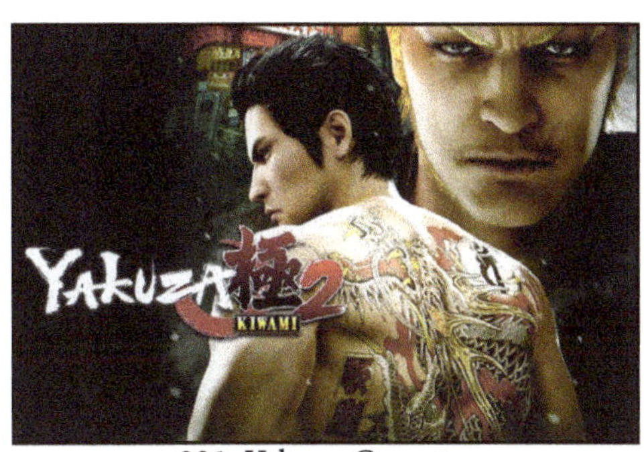

321. Yakuza Gangster

320. Movie Poster,
"The Fighting Seabees"

322. Royal Air Force Douglas C47 Dakota

323. Repulse Bay Hotel, Hong Kong,
Circa 1940s

ADDENDUM 2

Matthew Marne's Awards and Decorations

1. Navy Cross

2. Silver Star Medal

3. Legion of
Merit Medal

4. Bronze Star with V
and Two Stars

5. Meritorius
Service Medal

6. Purple Heart with
Four Clusters

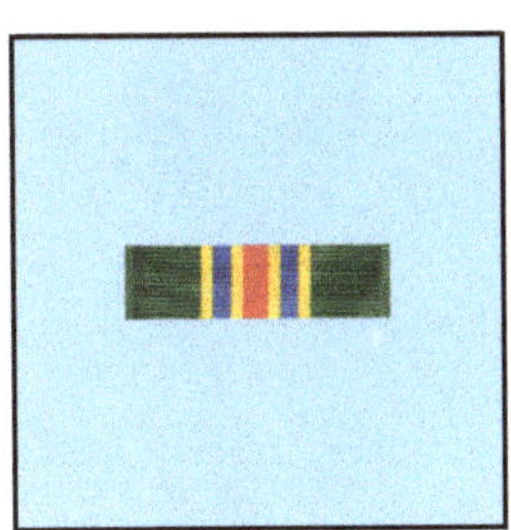

7. Navy Meritorious
Unit Commendation
Ribbon

Navy Good Conduct Medal
with Second Award Bar

9. Navy
Expedition Medal

10. China Service
Medal Navy

11. American Defense
Service Medal

12. Asiatic-Pacific
Campaign Medal

13. American
Campaign Medal

14. World War II
Victory Medal

15. Navy WW II
OccupationMedal

16. Nicaraguan
Campaign Medal

17. World War I Medal
with Destroyer Service Bar

18. Navy Pistol
Marksman Medal
with Expert Device

ADDENDUM 3

USS Panay's Ship's Company, Military Awards, and Civilian Passengers

Naval Officers

- Lieutenant Commander James J. Hughes, USN. Commanding Officer. *Distinguished Service Medal*
- Lieutenant Arthur "Tex" F. Anders, USN, Executive Officer. *Distinguished Service Medal.* (In 1969 the Navy changed Anders award to the Navy Cross.)
- Lieutenant Junior Grade, Clark G. Geist, USN, Gunnery Officer,
- Ensign, Dennis H. Biwerse, USN, Engineering Officer

Consular Officials

- George Atchison, First Secretary
- J. Hall Paxton, Second Secretary
- Madam Emilie Gassie, Clerk
- Captain, Frank N. Roberts, USA, Assistant Military Attaché. *Navy Cross*

Media Personnel

- Norman Alley, Universal News (newsreel cameraman)
- Luigi Barzini, Jr., *Corriere della Sera* (Milan daily newspaper)
- Jim Marshall, *Collier's Weekly*
- Eric Mayell, Movietone News (newsreel cameraman)
- Colin MacDonald, *Times of London*
- Sandro Sandri, *La Stampa* (Turin daily newspaper)

- Norman Soong, *The New York Times*
- James Weldon, United Press.

Civilians
- C. H. Carlson, Merchant Ship Master
- Rosi, H. Secretary, Italian Embassy
- Roy Squires, China Importing and Exporting, Ltd.
- F. H. Vines, British American Tobacco

Enlisted Personnel
- Adams, Charles S., Radioman, Second Class. *Navy Cross*
- Babpa, Tony, Supply Clerk, Third Class
- Birk, Carl H., Engineman, First Class
- Bonkoski, John A., Gunner's Mate, Third Class. *Navy Cross*
- Branch, Earnest C., Fireman, First Class
- Browning, Raymond L., Engineman, Third Class
- Cheathman, Walter C. Coxswain. *Navy Cross*
- Coleman, Thomas A., Chief Photographer' Mate
- Cowden, Edward E., Coxswain. *Navy Cross*
- Davis, Newton L., Fire Control Technician, First Class
- Dirnhoffer, John A., Seaman. *Navy Cross*
- Ducey, T. Messman
- Erh, Yuan T., Messman First Class. *Letter of Commendation*
- Fichtenmayer, Fred C., Boatswain Mate First Class
- Ensminger, Charles L., First Class Storekeeper
- Fisher, Emery F., Chief Machinist Mate
- Fong Sunk, King, Messman. *Bronze Star*
- Gerent, Michael., Machinist Mate, Second Class
- Green, C. B., Seaman
- Graizer, Clark G., Pharmacist Mate, First Class
- Halhmann, Earnest P. Chief Boatswain Mate
- Hebart, Robert P., Fireman First Class. *Navy Cross*
- Hennessy, John H., Gunner's Mate Second Class. *Navy Cross*

- Hodge, John L., Fireman First Class. *Navy Cross*
- Hoyle, W. T., Machinist Mate, Second Class
- Huffman, Fon B., Water tender Second Class. X?
- Hulsebus, Edgar W., Coxswain. *Navy Cross, posthumously*
- Johnson, Carl H., Machinist Mate Second Class
- Kerske, Carl H., Coxswain. *Navy Cross*
- Klulepears, P. H. , Chief Machinist Mate
- Kozak, Alex, Machinist Mate, Second Class. *Navy Cross*
- Lang, John H., Chief Quartermaster. *Navy Cross*
- Lander, William P., Seaman
- Lumpers, Peter H., Chief Machinist Mate
- Mahlmamm, Ernest R., Chief Boatswain Mate. *Navy Cross*
- Matt, Juan T., Electrician's Mate First Class
- McCabe, William A., Fireman First Class
- McEowen, Stanley W., Seaman. *Navy Cross*
- Murphy, James T., Radioman Third Class. *Navy Cross*
- Newton, Davis L., Fireman First Class
- Peck, James H., Quartermaster Second Class
- Peterson, Reginald P., Radioman Second Class. *Navy Cross*
- Puckett, Vernon F., Chief Machinist Mate
- Rice, Kenneth J., Engineman, Third Class
- Rider, Morris, Coxswain. *Navy Cross*
- Rinaldi, A. Seaman
- Schroyer, Charles S., Seaman
- Speen, Cecil B., Seaman
- Spindle, T. M. , Quartermaster, Third Class
- Sung, King P., Machinist Mate Second Class
- Tenny, J. P., Coxswain

ADDENDUM 4

Ship's Company and Civilian Casualties

Ship's Company Killed

- Coxswain Edgar W. Hulsebus. *Navy Cross, posthumously*
- First Class Storekeeper, Charles L. Ensminger.

Civilian Killed

- Sandro Sandri, *La Stampa* (Turin daily newspaper)

Note: All 74 personnel on board the *Panay* were wounded in some manner. Forty-three were serious.

Officers Wounded

- Lieutenant Commander James J. Hughes, USN. Commanding Officer.
- Lieutenant Arthur "Tex" F. Anders, USN, Executive Officer
- Lieutenant Junior Grade, Clark G. Geist, USN, Gunnery Officer
- Ensign, Dennis H. Biwerse, USN, Engineering Officer

Consular Officials Wounded

- J. Hall Paxton, Second Secretary
- Madam Emilie Gassie, Clerk

Media Personnel Wounded

- Norman Alley, Universal News (newsreel cameraman)
- Eric Mayell, Movietone News (newsreel cameraman)
- Colin MacDonald, *Times of London*

- Norman Soong, *The New York Times*
- Jim Marshall, **Collier's Weekly**
- Luigi Barzini, Jr., *Corriere della Sera* (Milan daily newspaper)

Enlisted Wounded

- Adams, Charles S., Radioman, Second Class
- Babpa, Tony, Supply Clerk, Third Class
- Birk, Carl H., Engineman, First Class
- Bonkoski, John A., Gunner's Mate, Third Class
- Branch, Earnest C., Fireman, First Class
- Browning, Raymond L., Engineman, Third Class
- Cheathman, Walter C. Coxswain
- Davis, Newton L., Fire Control Technician, First Class
- Dirnhoffer, John A., Seaman
- Erh, Yuan T., Messman First Class
- Fichtenmayer, Fred C., Boatswain Mate First Class
- Fisher, Emery F., Chief Machinist Mate
- Fong Sunk, King, Messman
- Halhmann, Earnest P. Chief Boatswain Mate
- Hebart, Robert P., Fireman First Class
- Johnson, Carl H., Machinist Mate Second Class
- Kozak, Alex, Machinist Mate, Second Class
- Lang, John H., Chief Quartermaster
- McCabe, William A., Fireman First Class
- McEowen, Stanley W., Seaman
- Peterson, Reginald P., Radioman Second Class
- Puckett, Vernon F., Chief Machinist Mate
- Rice, Kenneth J., Engineman, Third Class
- Rider, Morris, Coxswain
- Schroyer, Charles S., Seaman
- Sung, King P., Machinist Mate Second Class
- Tuck, Harry B., Signalman First Class
- Waxler, Cleo E., Boatswain Mate Second Class

- Weber, John H., Yeoman First Class
- Wong, Far Z., Machinist Mate First Class
- Ziegler, Peres D., Supply Clerk Third Class

HISTORICAL BACKGROUND

*D*ear reader, to set the perspective for this *roman à clef*, I've developed a brief review of the historical background of the Far East at the time of this narrative.

On Sunday, at 1338 hours on 12 December 1937, in an unprovoked attack, Japanese naval airplanes bombed and strafed the *United States Ship Panay*—sinking it, killing two sailors, and wounding most of its crew. The *Panay*, a ship in the Asiatic Fleet, was a gunboat on patrol on the Yangtze. When the Japanese attacked, the *Panay* was anchored about twenty-eight miles upriver from Nanking. At that time, the Second Sino-Japanese War (July 1937 to September 1945) was raging. The United States was a neutral in this war. However, our gunboats, and those of Great Britain, patrolled the Yangtze and Yellow Rivers to protect our citizens and our commercial interests.

By and large, the tragedy of the *USS Panay* has slipped into the files of ancient history. Yet, it was the opening gambit in the War in the Pacific (1941 to 1945). I was a nipper at the time. I remember the incident clearly, and was confident that this unprovoked Japanese attack on one of our warships would precipitate the Pacific war we knew was inevitable. Thankfully, President Roosevelt knew that the United States was woefully unprepared for war, and diplomatically asked the Japanese for an apology (mistake) and monetary compensation. The Japanese government responded with a $2.2 million-dollar indemnity. The president accepted this offer and the incident was officially closed.

Significantly, a full-scale Japanese attack occurred on our battle fleet at Pearl Harbor on 7 December 1941—almost four years to the day after their surprise attack on the *Panay*.

ABOUT THE AUTHOR

Captain S. Martin Shelton retired from active and reserve naval service with the rank of captain. He served in the Korean and Vietnamese Wars, and elsewhere as a combat motion-picture cameraman, photographic officer, and intelligence specialist. He has an extensive background in Far Eastern studies.

Shelton earned his Master of Arts Degree (Cinema) at the University of Southern California. He concentrated his studies on communications analysis, information theory, and film scripting and production.

For thirty years, he produced a host of information and documentary motion-media shows, winning over forty awards in national and international film competitions and festivals. His peers elected him a Fellow of the Society for Technical Communication and served as the President of the Information Film Producers of America.

After retirement, he began writing and publishing historical action-adventure novels set in the Far East and Africa. On the whole, his plots focus on important, yet little remembered, historical events of the early twentieth century. His writings comprise a mélange of aviators, assassins, and adventurers. His novella titled Khartoum earned a Finalist Award in the Writer's League of Texas annual publication competition, and his novella Abyssinia earned a Finalist Award in the National INDIE Excellence Awards.

Shelton has posted details of his literary work at sheltoncomm.com.

www.ingramcontent.com/pod-product-compliance
Lightning Source LLC
Chambersburg PA
CBHW041745010726
47507CB00008B/295